DESERT CROSSING

Elise Broach is the author of the acclaimed novel *Shakespeare's Secret*, as well as several picture books. She did graduate work in history at Yale University, and her non-fiction research and writing projects have taken her to the deserts of the American Southwest several times.

Elise lives with her husband and three children in Easton, Connecticut, where she writes, edits the library newsletter and is active in town government.

Visit her at **www.elisebroach.com**

Books by the same author

Shakespeare's Secret

DESERT CROSSING

ELISE BROACH

WALKER BOOKS
AND SUBSIDIARIES

LONDON · BOSTON · SYDNEY · AUCKLAND

This is a work of fiction. Names, characters, places and incidents are
either the product of the author's imagination or, if real, are used fictitiously.

Published by arrangement with Henry Holt and Company LLC.

This edition published 2007 by Walker Books Ltd
87 Vauxhall Walk, London SE11 5HJ

2 4 6 8 10 9 7 5 3

Text © 2006 Elise Broach

Woman wearing sunglasses image: Tom Morrison/Getty Images
Desert Highway in Pecos Texas image © Royalty-Free/Corbis

The right of Elise Broach to be identified as author of this work has been asserted
by her in accordance with the Copyright, Designs and Patents Act 1988

This book has been typeset in M Bembo

Printed in Great Britain by Cox & Wyman Ltd, Reading, Berkshire

All rights reserved. No part of this book may be reproduced, transmitted
or stored in an information retrieval system in any form or by any means, graphic,
electronic or mechanical, including photocopying, taping
and recording, without prior written permission from the publisher.

British Library Cataloguing in Publication Data:
a catalogue record for this book
is available from the British Library

ISBN 978-1-4063-0368-1

www.walkerbooks.co.uk

For my brother and sister,
Mark and Mary Broach,
with thanks for many shared adventures

1

There are some kinds of trouble you never see coming, like those thunderstorms that start from nothing at all. One minute the sky is blue and distant. Then, all of a sudden, it's dark and thick with clouds, pressing down right on top of you. The leaves turn silvery and twist in the wind, the air starts to hum, and the rain comes, so heavy and fast you can't even see. You almost never make it to the house in time.

That's how it was the night we drove through New Mexico. It had been sunny all day, too hot in the car, and I was sticky with sweat, sick of the back seat, sick of the way Kit kept turning the front air vents so they all faced him. My brother, Jamie, was driving, and he let Kit do whatever he liked. He thought it was funny.

"Come on," I kept saying. "Can I get a little air back

here?" I plucked my T-shirt away from my skin and fanned my stomach. "I'm going to pass out."

"Go ahead," Kit said. "We could use the quiet."

Jamie just laughed, so I kicked the back of his seat, hard. Then he whipped the steering wheel from side to side so the whole car shook, saying, "Cut it out, Luce. You'll be sorry."

We were driving from Kansas City to Phoenix to spend spring break with my dad. Don't ask me why Kit had to come. He was Jamie's best friend, and his parents had gone to the Bahamas "to work on their marriage." This is exactly the kind of thing you don't want to hear about somebody else's parents, although I guess it's better than hearing it about your own. Our parents were divorced already, so Jamie and I didn't have to deal with stuff like that. But it was something that never made sense to me: how a relationship could be separate from the two people in it, its own living, breathing thing.

Anyway, Kit had nothing better to do for spring break and decided to come with us. It changed the whole trip. I was stuck in the back seat, which was bad enough, but on top of that, I had to listen to the two of them talk about girls for twelve hours straight, all the way across Kansas, Oklahoma, part of Texas, and now New Mexico.

It started with Jamie saying something like, "Did you see Maddie Dilworth at the gym on Saturday?" Kit banged his fist on the dashboard and said, "Oh, yeah! Yeah. She's *hot*."

And then, like I wasn't even there, they proceeded to

8

discuss every single part of Maddie Dilworth's body. Which was interesting for, maybe, three seconds. I sat with my sketchbook on my lap, trying to draw, but sweat dripped on the page and blurred the lines. I couldn't concentrate. I kept looking at my skinny legs – too white – and the way my shirt puddled over my chest. I would be fifteen in a month but I always felt younger when I was with Jamie and Kit – more like twelve. They kept right on talking, about another girl at the gym, then a junior who worked at Kane's Drugs, then Kristi Bendall, a girl in my grade. They were seniors! I couldn't take it anymore.

"Hello? She's a freshman, you jerks. Isn't that too young for you? She's in my math class! I don't want to hear what you think of her boobs. Can you stop, please?"

"Lighten up," Kit said. Jamie just laughed.

I reached between them to crank up the radio. I spread out the map, tenting it over the seat. I interrupted them every time I saw a road sign. But it didn't matter. They were on a roll, and I was doomed.

"This is the most boring car ride of my life," I said.

Kit snorted. "Like we care?"

That's the kind of guy he was. If he didn't have some use for you, you might as well not be there at all.

The whole trip was like that. Every time we stopped at a diner, he and Jamie sat at a table by themselves so they could hit on the waitresses. "Hey, how's it going? What's the best thing on the menu? No, you pick. Bring us your favorite. We trust you."

That sounds so stupid you'd think the waitresses would ignore them. But they're cute, both of them, which is why they get away with it. Jamie and I look like our dad – dark eyes, straight nose, big smile – and Kit has reddish hair that's so soft and wavy you can't help but want to touch it. Until you get to know him.

The women weren't that pretty, mostly. They had dyed hair and brown teeth and those husky smokers' voices. But they smiled a lot and shot long, sly looks at Jamie and Kit, and that was all it took. Jamie loved women, and Kit ... well, as my mom would say, Kit loved the sound of his own voice.

So I had to watch them smirk and hold open doors and leave extra bills every place we stopped. At the last restaurant, the waitress was Mexican and barely spoke English. They fell all over themselves with their high school Spanish – *por favor, claro que sí, no más* – trying to impress her. Our dad is half Mexican and fluent in Spanish, so Jamie could fake it better than Kit, but even so, they kept screwing up. The waitress just laughed at them.

I clapped my headphones over my ears and drew pictures on the thin paper place mat: a cactus and a coyote, then the waitress, with her wide, smooth forehead and the dark swoops of her eyebrows. I kept wishing for my best friend, Ginny. If she were there, we would be cracking up, making fun of Jamie and Kit. But without her, all I could do was try to look busy, not like some loser eating all by herself.

I was tired of being ignored.

So now, back in the hot car, I was arguing with Kit to make him change places with me.

"Come on, you've been up there the whole trip. It's not fair. This isn't even your car. I'm too hot!"

"Then have something to drink." Kit bent down and snapped open the six-pack at his feet. He'd gotten it from a trucker, talked him into buying it so he and Jamie wouldn't get caught.

"Hey!" I said. "What are you doing?"

Kit handed Jamie a beer and took one for himself. "I'm thirsty." He turned and pressed the cold can against my arm. I flinched, and he grinned.

I shoved his hand away. "You said those were for Albuquerque, for the hotel. Jamie, jeez, Mom would kill you. Not while you're driving. What if a cop stops us?"

Jamie's eyes flashed in the rearview mirror. "There aren't any cops around here."

He was right. There was nothing but desert, reddish and gravelly, rolling for miles in every direction. Kansas was flat, too, but not like this. It was greener, softer, with dense clusters of houses nudging up against farmland. This place was empty. We passed scatterings of rocks and scrub brush, and in the distance I could see a ragged line of mountains, blue and faint. But other than that, only the dry, hard ground, with its shocks of silvery grass, cartoon-ish paddle-leaved cactus, and the dark surprise of shrubs. All afternoon I'd been thinking how strange it was that somebody put a road here, as if a road could make this someplace worth going. Jamie'd gotten off the main highway hours ago because he said it was boring.

I gave Jamie's seat another kick, just to bug him.

"Cut it out, Luce. Look, it's not even hot now."

He was right. It was almost dark. Suddenly the sky turned a thick, angry gray. I rolled down the window and leaned my face into the rush of wind, my hair whipping my cheeks. The air was gusty, turning cooler. It roared through the car.

That's when it started to rain.

"Put up the windows!" Jamie yelled.

The rain spilled from the sky, a torrent of it, slamming the roof of the car and gushing across the highway. The windshield blurred. The road disappeared.

I grabbed Jamie's headrest. "Slow down!"

"Wooo-hoooo!" Kit threw back his head. "This is amazing!"

It was like being underwater, streaking through an ocean, dark and black.

Then we felt it.

A bump.

Big, but hollow, too. A kind of thunking as the car hit something.

2

My knees bumped the front seat, and Jamie's beer sloshed over the dashboard.

"Damn," Jamie said.

He braked, jerking the wheel. Then the car started to slide, and he sped up again, trying to control it.

"Hey, easy," Kit said. "Whatever it was, you hit it."

"What?" I cried. "What was it?" I scrambled onto my knees and squinted through the rear window. In the red glow of the taillights, through the pouring rain, I could see something dark in the road. It jerked and spasmed, then crawled off to the side. "Oh my God, Jamie! You hit something! It's in the road. What was it?"

"I don't know." Jamie's voice was shaking. "Maybe a coyote. It ran right into the bumper. I didn't have time to brake."

He was driving more slowly now. His hands were clenched and pale on the steering wheel. The rain seemed to wash away the night in front of us and behind. I couldn't see anything.

"But it was still alive," I said. "We have to go back."

Kit turned around. "What for? It's just some animal."

I kept peering through the rear window, through the silvery curtain of water. "But what if it's a dog?"

"Nobody lives around here. How could it be a dog?"

And that would have been it, end of discussion, because I wasn't sure, and Jamie was shaken, and Kit was impatient, and Albuquerque was still an hour away. That would have been it, if I hadn't seen the patch of yellow light – a wet, bright smudge in the middle of the desert.

"No, wait!" I cried. "There's a house. It could be a dog. It could be somebody's dog! Jamie, come on. We have to go back."

Kit whipped around. "Are you kidding me? What are we going to do? Nothing! It was an accident. He ran straight into the frigging road."

But Jamie was already braking. He heaved the car into reverse and swiveled around on the highway.

"What are you doing?" Kit glared at him, disgusted.

"I'm going back." My brother's voice was quiet but certain, like somebody had asked him a question he shouldn't have to answer. We were crazy about dogs in my family. Kit knew it, too. He made a big show of shaking his head and rolling his eyes, but he knew we had to go back.

The road looked strange in the dark. It was slick and flooded with water that shone in the headlights. Jamie drove more slowly. We couldn't tell how far we'd come. I kept my face pressed to the window, watching every shape along the road: the mile-marker posts, the scraggly bushes, the sudden, looming boulders. I was staring so hard my eyes hurt. The night was almost black now, and we were pushing through rain that fell so fast it seemed as solid as a wall.

"We're not going to find anything," Kit said, tapping his foot noisily against the dashboard. And a minute later, "See? It's gone. Maybe you just clipped it. We've gone too far already. Turn around."

But then I saw it: something shadowy and unexpected, lying near the side of the road.

"Jamie! Stop! It's over there."

Jamie braked, and the car skidded sideways. "Where? What?"

"Look." I pointed, but through the rain, I couldn't be sure.

"You're both crazy," Kit said. "I can't believe we're doing this. So what if it is a dog? It's probably, like, rabid. What are we going to do with it?"

"I don't know," Jamie mumbled. "But come on, let's take a look." He turned the car again and pulled across the road, shining the headlights where I'd been pointing. A white arc of light covered the road. I swung open the car door and the blast of wet air made me shiver. There were jackets buried somewhere in the trunk, but Jamie and Kit just pulled their T-shirts on top of their heads and stumbled into the rain. It washed over us, drenching our clothes, sending rivers down our arms and legs. With their shirts surrounding their faces, Jamie and Kit looked like ghosts.

I ran ahead.

"There it is!" I yelled. I heard the crunch of Jamie's feet on the gravel behind me.

In the glare of the headlights, I could see it. Something pale, curving away from the road.

I stopped where I was. Jamie almost knocked into me. We stood there, staring. We couldn't breathe.

It wasn't an animal.

It was a girl, her slim arm curving across the gravel, like a ballerina's. *Oh my God,* I thought.

3

There are moments when everything changes, and it happens so quickly, in the time it takes to blink or catch your breath. It's like there's a line between "then" and "now," and you can feel yourself stepping over it, and you don't want to because you know you can't go back. That's how it was when we saw the girl. We walked toward her, with Kit coming up behind us, and I don't know how we did it, how we moved our feet or remembered to breathe. I wanted to run back to the car, wanted to grab their hands and pull them with me, back into the minute before this minute, so we could drive away into the night without knowing. Because knowing would change everything. As soon as we saw her, I could feel it: We were walking away from our old life and into something else.

When we got to her, we could see her hair flowing over the ground in a wet, dark fan. Her eyes were wide open, unblinking in the rain. She was dead.

None of us said anything. We stood there with the rain pouring all around us and looked at that girl, looked and looked at her, as if we could somehow stare the life back into her, get her up on her feet, away from the road, away from cars in the rain.

I'd never seen a dead person before. I kept thinking, if this were a movie, people would be frantic now, checking her pulse, stretching her flat, pounding her chest. And maybe after a minute, she'd cough or wheeze, and you'd know she was going to be okay. But this girl was so still. Even in the roar of the storm, you could feel the quiet space around her.

Jamie squatted next to her. "But it was a coyote," he said slowly.

Kit bent over, hands on his knees. He gave a long, shuddering breath. "It was dark. You couldn't see. She came right into the road."

"No," Jamie said. "It was an animal."

"You couldn't see."

"No."

"Jamie..." I touched his shoulder. He shook his head hard, jerking away from me. I couldn't take my eyes off the girl. Her mouth was partly open, a small, clean oval, utterly silent. She was older than we were, but not by much. Everything about her was ordinary: dark jeans, a

18

T-shirt with writing across the front, a silver charm bracelet that looked like the one I had in my top drawer at home. Her nail polish was chipping. One ear was double-pierced. How could she be dead?

Her body lay at an angle, twisted, with her shirt hiked up, showing a band of pale skin. I reached out and pulled the shirt down. Then − I don't know why − I felt sick, completely sick, and I started throwing up. In the middle of it, as I was doubled over, I felt someone grab my hair and gather it back from my face. It must have been Kit, which was strange, but not stranger than anything else.

Jamie yanked his T-shirt back off his head, and the rain poured over him, plastering his hair to his forehead. He didn't look at me. "It's okay, Luce. We'll call somebody."

"Here," Kit said, taking out his cell phone. He shielded it from the rain with his palm, turning and pointing it in different directions, punching the keypad. Finally he looked up hopelessly. "There's no signal."

And then I remembered. "There was a house," I said.

"What?" They both turned to me.

"That light we saw. We can get help."

"Yeah, okay," Jamie said. Something in his face was different, closed off. He kept staring at the girl. "She's too near the road. Can we move her away?"

Kit shook his head. "I don't think we should touch her."

I swallowed hard. "What if somebody hits her? What if somebody runs over her?"

"She's dead," Kit said.

Jamie's mouth was a tight line, but his eyes were huge. "I'll stay here. You guys drive to the house. I'll wait with her."

Kit frowned. "There's nothing you can do."

Jamie threw him the car keys. "Just go."

So Kit and I went back to the car. Kit opened the trunk and tossed me my jacket, but I just stood there looking at it in my hands. I couldn't think what to do.

"Put it on," he said. And then I realized I was shaking. We got in the car, and I held Jamie's windbreaker out the window for him as we rolled slowly past. Jamie took it and flopped it over one shoulder, the rain still gusting around him. I watched him in the rearview mirror as we drove away. He got darker and smaller, but I could still see the jacket, flapping uselessly, like a flag.

4

It was raining so hard we could barely see the turnoff. But the light was there, deep in the desert blackness, and when we slowed down we saw a thin gravel lane breaking off from the highway. It was muddy and pooled with water. Little streams coursed over it. Kit slowed the car to a crawl, and we bumped and heaved over the ruts. I was still shivering, but I felt like I was waking up, paying more attention. Now everything seemed too real: the metal handle of the car door, ice cold, pushed against my thigh, and the tangy smell of beer filled the front seat. I kept sneaking quick looks at Kit. It wasn't like him not to talk.

Finally he said, "We should get rid of the cans."

"What?"

"We have to dump the beer."

"Now?"

It seemed impossible that there was something else to think of besides the girl. But there would be police.

"I don't know," I said.

"We have to get rid of it."

"But the car really smells. They'll figure it out. It'll look like…" I didn't know how to say it.

Kit shrugged, squinting at the road. "If they find open beer cans in the car…" He hesitated. "Think about Jamie."

I was mad at him, furious. He was the one who'd wanted the beer, gotten the six-pack, given Jamie a can while he was driving. And now a girl was dead, and it wasn't Jamie's fault, it couldn't be Jamie's fault. But we'd been driving fast and our car stank of beer. Who would know what really happened?

"I *am* thinking about Jamie," I said. Kit shot me a side-ways glance. He slowed the car and rolled down his window. Then he reached across my shins and grabbed the two cans, heaving them into the night. A minute later, he sent the rest of the six-pack spiraling after them.

"Kit," I said. But he just drove on.

Suddenly the house was in front of us. It was low and rambling, with lights shining in two of the windows. There was a truck parked next to it. As soon as we pulled into the yard – if you could call it a yard because there wasn't a boundary, it stretched right into the desert – two big dogs came charging out of a shed, barking.

We stepped out into the rain.

The dogs surrounded Kit, but their big tails swished back and forth, and they only sniffed his legs. I pulled up my hood and headed for the door.

It opened before I had a chance to knock. A woman in her thirties stood there, wearing a man's shirt spattered with paint. She had a pretty face, tan from the sun, and her dark hair fell around it like a veil. She brushed it back, looking annoyed. "Yes? What is it? Car trouble?"

"No," I said. "There's ... we..." I couldn't think what to say.

Kit came running up then, with the dogs bounding beside him and tangling in his legs.

"Oscar! Toronto!" the woman said sharply. The dogs backed away, cringing. I held out my hand to the big black one, and he licked it, butting his head under my palm.

Kit was talking fast. "A girl ran into the road. Right in front of our car. She's ... she's dead. My friend stayed back there with her, but she's dead."

The woman looked from Kit to me. She had dark, steady eyes, and it was hard to look back at her. "Come inside," she said. "I'll call the police."

We dripped water all over the floor while she dialed. There was, in the middle of the room, a huge piece of twisted metal, painted all different colors, with weird things sticking out of it – a hubcap, a piece of pipe. A drop cloth was spread underneath it, and a rug was rolled up against the wall. Kit looked at me and raised his eyebrows.

"Joe? Hi, it's Beth Osway. I've got a couple of kids here. They've had an accident, they hit somebody. They think she might be dead." She listened for a minute, then turned to Kit. "Where was it? How far from my road?"

Kit gestured. "I don't know, east of here, maybe two, three miles?"

She repeated the information into the phone. "Okay, we'll meet them there." She turned to us. "Are you all right? Were either of you hurt?"

We shook our heads.

"No, they seem to be fine." She hung up and took a nylon jacket from a peg on the wall. "It'll take them a while," she said. "But we'll go wait."

She looked at us curiously then, with the same sharp gaze, almost like she was solving a puzzle. "I'm Beth. What are your names?"

Kit spoke. "Kit Kitson and Lucy Martinez."

She looked at Kit. "Kit Kitson?"

Kit flushed. "Well, Frederick. But everybody calls me Kit."

I stared at him. Frederick? I wasn't sure even Jamie knew that.

We ran out into the rain again. When I climbed into the back of the car, the smell of beer was stronger than ever. Beth pulled open the passenger door and started to get in, but she stopped. She looked around the inside of the car, then back at me.

"Have you been drinking?"

"No!" I said quickly. "No ... I'm only fourteen."

Kit was sliding into the front seat, not looking at her.

Her eyes didn't move from my face. "Has he been drinking?"

I turned to Kit. He started the car, not saying anything.

Beth reached over and twisted the keys, yanking them out of the ignition. "We'll take the truck," she said. Her voice was hard.

5

In the truck, I sat in the middle, pulling my shoulders together so I wouldn't have to touch either of them. I could feel Kit shifting around, getting ready to say something. In the dark cab, his face looked tense; the usual smirk had disappeared.

"We weren't drinking," he said finally.

Beth didn't answer. I stared at him. I couldn't believe he was going to lie. She'd been inside the stinking car.

Kit shrugged. "I mean, we had one beer."

Beth kept her eyes on the road. The windshield wipers swished back and forth in a panic, beating in time with my heart.

Kit leaned forward. "Like one sip, really. Half of it spilled, anyway. You know, when we…" He was trying to get her to look at him, but her eyes stayed on the road.

She frowned. "Pretty goddamn stupid, don't you think?"

Kit sank back, defeated, and I shrank into myself. I couldn't figure her out. She seemed to be helping us, sort of, by calling the police and driving us back to Jamie. But she wasn't treating us the way a normal adult would. She didn't keep asking us questions to fill the gaps in the conversation. She just seemed eager to get rid of us.

Then we saw Jamie, sitting where we'd left him.

"There he is," I said softly, but Beth had already seen him and was slowing the truck, steering onto the shoulder.

"Stay here," she said abruptly, slamming the door. I scooted away from Kit and watched through the window. She walked over to Jamie, pulling up her hood. He tried to stand but his legs were unsteady. He looked like he hadn't moved since we left. He stumbled sideways and Beth grabbed his arm to keep him from falling.

I could see him talking to her, her answering. He pointed at the girl. Beth squatted down and stayed there awhile, with Jamie gesturing and talking. When she started to get back up, he held out his hand to help her.

"What are they talking about?" Kit asked.

"I don't know." I glanced over at him. "Maybe the beer you didn't drink."

"Oh, come on. What was I supposed to say? We're in enough trouble without her making a federal case out of that. It wasn't even half a can."

"But you can smell it in the car! It's just dumb to lie about it now."

27

"Okay, okay." He looked mad. "I didn't hear you come up with any great ideas."

There was nothing I could say to that.

I turned back to the window, and as suddenly as it had begun, the rain stopped. It didn't taper off to a drizzle – it stopped altogether. We sat in the new silence, listening to the tiny trickling sounds of water streaming off the road. The windshield sparkled with a screen of droplets. The highway shone like a river in the headlights. I could barely look at the girl. What had she been doing out here, alone, on the road? I opened the door and the damp night air swept into the truck, making me shiver.

We could hear Jamie's voice, muted, talking to Beth. Maybe she was asking him about the beer. He'd tell her the whole truth, I was pretty sure. He wasn't like Kit that way. He wouldn't be thinking ahead and trying to guess the consequences.

"Look," Kit said, pointing. In the distance I could see tiny flashes of red and blue light streaking across the land. In almost the same minute, we heard the whine of sirens. My arms shook. I clutched my elbows to hold them still.

What would happen to us? People went to jail for things like this. Drunk driving, hitting and killing someone. Wasn't it murder? But Jamie wasn't drunk. Kit was right. They didn't drink much at all. I hoped Kit couldn't see how I was trembling.

Beth came back to the truck and rested her hand on the door. "Here they come. You might as well get out."

We walked over to Jamie. He was sopping wet, his T-shirt so drenched it stuck to his chest, transparent. His hair hung down over his eyes and he flipped it back, spraying water on us.

"There hasn't been one car since you left," he said. "It's freaky out here."

We could hear the night rustling, close to us, except for the hushed patch of gravel where the girl lay.

Kit jerked his head. "Can we stand over there? Away from this?"

"Her," I said.

Kit walked a few yards away, and Jamie and Beth followed. I stayed where I was. I crouched down to really look at her. Her eyes were as shiny and light as glass. Her cheeks glistened. She had no expression at all. It was different from the way people looked when they were sleeping. So much blanker than that, with no flicker or twitch, no sign that her face would ever change.

Her T-shirt was dark blue. Letters stretched across it in big, excited loops: THE ROCKIES ROCK! Maybe she was from Colorado. Or she'd gone there on vacation. Or somebody brought her this T-shirt back from a trip.

The sirens were getting louder. I looked at her curled white hand, at the bracelet circling her wrist. Shouldn't it be easier to destroy a bracelet than a person? Shouldn't that be the first thing that got crushed or shattered? But the bracelet was perfect, exactly as it had been when she was alive.

It looked like my charm bracelet at home. It had a silver heart hanging from it, just like mine. Someone would take her away soon. This bracelet would be all that was left.

It seemed so unfair. Something should stay.

Before I even thought about what I was doing, I reached out and unclasped it, sliding it under her arm. The tips of my fingers grazed her cold skin, and the charms jangled against each other. I knew it was wrong. I could hardly breathe. I didn't know why I was doing it.

I shoved it deep inside my jacket pocket just as the police cars came screaming to a stop.

6

There were three cops. They got out of their cars all at once, with the ambulance wailing behind them. The paramedics swung open its back doors and yanked a metal stretcher to the ground. It clattered across the road. Then they crouched by the girl, and their hands were quick and confident, lifting her wrist, feeling her neck, shining a tiny, piercing light in her eyes. The police had flashlights. They walked around, looking at the road and the gravel shoulder where she was lying. Somebody took pictures, and the fierce burst of the flash made me blink. They talked to the paramedics. They marked the outline of her body. Everyone seemed to know what to do.

I watched the paramedics move the girl onto the stretcher. They straightened her out and pressed her arms close to her sides. For a minute, it seemed like they were

31

tucking her in, the way my mom sometimes did when I was almost asleep, smoothing the covers, and if my arm dropped over the edge of the mattress, sliding it back toward the middle.

But then they snapped the white sheet taut and covered her completely.

One cop stayed at the ambulance, and the other two walked toward us. Watching them come, with their shiny badges and bulging holsters, I felt a wave of fear wash through me. The girl had been alive, and now she was dead. There was nothing between those two moments but us. My heart started to pound. We'd done something terrible. Even if it was an accident, there was no way it wasn't our fault.

A heavy, older man, the one who seemed to be in charge, came up to us. He rubbed his forehead and nodded to Beth. "How have you been, Beth? I haven't seen you in a while."

"Fine, Stan. Busy. How about you?" Beth tossed her hair back, staring at the ambulance.

"Not too bad. It's a shame about that girl. She's young."

"I know, I know." Beth shook her head. "What was she doing out here, by herself? Did you pass any breakdowns?"

"Nope, nothing reported from here to Kilmore." He turned to us. "I'm Sheriff Durrell," he said. "We'll need to get statements from you folks. Now, which of you was the driver?"

Jamie nodded slightly, biting his lip.

"And where's your vehicle?"

"It's at my house," Beth said. "Let me talk to you for a minute, Stan."

She pulled him away from us, speaking softly. I could hear Kit swearing under his breath. Jamie shook his head. "Cut it out, Kit. We've got to tell them what happened. Okay? Everything that happened."

Kit frowned. "I don't even know what happened. Do you?"

Then the sheriff came back, and he was different, bristling and curt. "I understand you boys have been drinking. Can I see your licenses? We'll need to run a few checks. And how about you, young lady? Did you have any alcohol this evening?"

"No," I said quickly, but I couldn't look at him. I could feel the weight of the bracelet in my pocket.

"Are you aware the legal drinking age is twenty-one?"

"She didn't have any," Jamie said.

When I raised my eyes, the sheriff was still watching me. "Walk that way, toward the squad car, in a straight line," he ordered. "Heel to toe, arms at your sides, count the steps out loud."

I felt my cheeks get hot. I did what he said, placing my feet carefully. "One, two, three..." My voice was thin and high.

"Louder," he said. I swallowed. I couldn't stand all of them watching me. "Eight, nine..."

"Okay, that's enough," he called. "Come on back. What's your name?"

"Lucy Martinez."

"Roy!"

I jumped.

"Take Miss Martinez back to the car and get her statement." He turned to Jamie and Kit. "You boys stay with me."

I followed the younger cop to the police car. As we walked away, I glanced back and saw Jamie and Kit standing like statues, arms pressed to their sides. It seemed not real and too real at the same time, like a dream. The sheriff was making each of them raise one leg out in front and hold it there. Another time it would have been funny— they looked like storks – but not now, with their faces stiff and scared. There was no way they were drunk. But I was afraid for them, even so.

The police car was dark inside, with a sharp, sour smell. What was it? Sweat? Blinking screens and gauges crowded the front panel. It looked like the controls for a spaceship. Staticky voices burst over the radio, making me flinch. The clock said 10:38.

"Is it that late?" I asked, and then felt stupid when he didn't answer. I realized I didn't have any sense of the time. I had no idea when we had the accident, when we got to Beth's, when the police arrived. Of course he would ask me that. And I wouldn't know.

The cop turned down the radio and took out a clipboard with a printed form on it. He asked questions without looking at me – my name, my address, my age – scribbling across the page in quick, dark lines. I watched the side of his face in the dim light of the car. A muscle in his jaw twitched under the skin. "Okay, tell me what happened."

I pressed my lips together and stared out the window, thinking hard. I would be careful, like Jamie said. I wanted to tell him everything. "We were driving—"

"Who was driving?"

"Jamie. My brother, Jamie."

"And you were in the front seat?"

"No … no, Kit was in front. I was in the back, behind Jamie. We're driving to Phoenix to see my dad, and we were trying to get to Albuquerque tonight, to break up the trip. It started to rain really hard."

"What time was that?"

I bit my lip. "I don't know. I didn't look at the clock."

"Roughly what time? Seven o'clock? Eight?"

"It was dark. I don't know. It could have been dark because of the storm, but I think it was after sunset. Maybe seven-thirty?"

"And how would you characterize the visibility?"

"Uh…"

"How well could you see the road?"

I thought of that ocean swirling around us. "It was raining hard," I said.

"So the visibility was poor?"

"Yes."

"And did your brother adjust his speed? Did he slow down?"

I thought of us racing through the dark, watery night. "I don't know. I wasn't paying attention."

"And then what happened?"

"We hit something."

"What did you hit?"

"I didn't see it. I just felt the bump."

"You didn't see it because you weren't looking out the front? Or because you were looking but you couldn't see what it was?"

I tried to think. Had I been looking through the windshield when we hit her? I couldn't remember now. The rain blurred everything.

"I don't know. I don't think I was looking out the front."

"Did your brother brake? Did the car skid?"

"No, no, it happened too fast. There wasn't time to brake."

He stopped writing. "But you weren't actually looking in front of the car. Is that right? So you don't know if there was time to brake."

I pushed my hand deeper inside my pocket and touched the bracelet. For a minute, it made me feel more scared. But then, somehow, safer. I closed my fist around it and took a deep breath.

"No, I guess not. But it happened quickly."

"After the bump, did your brother brake?"

"Yes, he braked. Yes."

"And stopped the car?"

"No, he thought it was an animal. A coyote."

"Did he say why he thought that?"

"I guess that's what he thought he saw."

"But you didn't see a coyote."

I shook my head. "But I looked back, afterwards, and I saw something in the road."

The cop turned toward me, interested. "What did you see?"

"It was dark, there was too much rain. I don't know."

"Well, did it look like an animal?"

"It could have been an animal."

"And it was in the road?"

I thought of the dark, spasming thing in the road, that injured, dying thing. I couldn't look at him. I tightened my fingers around the bracelet, and the sharp edges of the charms cut into my palm. "It was trying to get off the road."

"So it was moving?"

"Yes..."

"Upright? Or—?"

"No. Sort of crawling, close to the ground."

"So what you hit was still alive?"

I thought of her lying there, with her beautiful curving arm and her dark hair like a halo. I heard Jamie's voice: *But it was a coyote.*

"I guess," I whispered.

"What did you do at that point?"

"I told Jamie and Kit. I said I saw something move, and we talked about going back, and Kit thought if it was a wild animal there was nothing we could do."

The cop paused, holding his pen over the page. "Did you or your brother, or the other passenger, discuss that what you saw in the road might be a person?"

"No!" My throat ached. I sucked in my breath and clenched my fist around the bracelet. It hurt, but I was glad it hurt. "No. We never thought that. If we'd thought that, we would have stopped right away."

He was writing again, quick, certain words, even though everything I said was so unsure. He glanced over at me. "Miss Martinez, do you need to take a break for a few minutes?"

I shook my head.

"Tell me what happened next."

"We turned around. We went back, and when we got to the place, we found her there."

"And it was raining this entire time?"

"Yes."

"And what happened then?"

"We ... we saw right away that she was dead."

"How did you know she was dead?"

I chewed on my lip, hesitating. "We could tell. Her eyes were open. She wasn't moving or breathing or anything."

"Did you attempt to perform any kind of resuscitation on the victim?"

It was the first time anyone had called her that. I looked at him. If she was the victim, what were we?

"No. She was dead. But we tried to call 911. We couldn't get a signal on the cell phone."

"And what did you do then?"

I told him the rest, quickly, without stopping for air. Now that we'd gotten to the part where she was dead, nothing else really mattered. I told him how I'd thrown up, how we drove to Beth's to get help, how Jamie stayed behind. It seemed important to tell him that Jamie stayed behind. Like that was the one thing we'd done right.

He listened and wrote. Then a stuffy silence filled the car. I watched his face while he checked over his notes. I could draw it, I was thinking, the sharp line of his jaw. But I didn't know what it meant. Was he mad? Did he believe me?

People's faces were like that when you first started drawing them: geometrical, abstract. They became less familiar the longer you looked at them, segmenting into shapes like a puzzle, impossible to solve.

Finally he said, "All right, Miss Martinez, I think that's it. You must be pretty worn out." For the first time, he looked at me, really looked at me. He had nice eyes, crinkly at the corners. If I'd seen him playing baseball or walking his dog, I never would have thought he was a cop. He didn't seem like a person who spent his life around criminals and dead people.

I looked at the clock. It was almost midnight.

7

When I got back to Beth's truck, she was leaning against the hood talking to the sheriff. He was shaking his head.

"We have to take him back to the station. The mother's been contacted. The other one and the girl can go, but not the driver."

I craned around, panicking. Where was Jamie? They were going to take him away.

The cop put his hand on my shoulder. "It's okay," he said. "It's procedure. He's eighteen?"

I nodded mutely. Jamie and Kit were standing near one of the police cars. Kit was watching me, his eyes worried, but Jamie just stared at the ground. He kicked the dirt with his sneaker, his hands shoved deep in his pockets. I walked toward them.

I heard Beth ask the sheriff, "Where will they go?"

"Well, there's the motel in Kilmore, but that's pretty far for tonight. And we have to impound the vehicle. I could bring them back to the detention center. But…"

I turned back and Beth frowned, coiling the length of her hair. She sighed. "They can stay at my house, I guess. If it's only for the night. But do you have to get their car now? It's so late."

"Yeah. I'll send somebody to tow it. You can go on to bed." He gestured to me. "Miss Martinez? I'll have the station find out from your mother how she'd like us to handle things tonight."

I looked at Jamie. "What about my brother? I want to stay with him."

The sheriff shook his head. "I'm sorry, he needs to come with us."

This time Jamie raised his eyes, wide and worried. I could feel a sharpness in the back of my throat, and I was afraid I might burst into tears. "Can't we all stay together? Please?" I asked.

But the sheriff was already walking away, the heavy holster banging against his leg.

"What about our dad?" I asked Beth. "He's expecting us in Phoenix tomorrow night. Our spring break is only a week."

She came toward us, and her voice was gentler than before. "I don't think you guys are going anywhere any time soon."

Kit sucked in his breath. "Aw, come on, it was an accident. They can't charge us with anything. Well, the beer, yeah, but we weren't drunk – it wasn't our fault. I mean, if somebody walks straight in front of your car, at night, is it your fault? That doesn't make sense."

I could see Jamie ball his hand against his thigh. "Stop saying that. I didn't hit that girl. I keep telling you. What I hit, it wasn't a person."

"Okay, okay," Kit said quickly. "Relax. I'm just saying that's what the cops think. And even if it was the girl, there wasn't time to brake or swerve or anything. I told them that. There was nothing you could do."

"It was an animal," Jamie said. "It was a coyote."

Beth put her hand on Jamie's arm. There were tiny flecks of green paint on her knuckles. "Don't think about it anymore. Whatever happened, you can't change it now."

Jamie stared at her fingers. He didn't say anything.

She let go abruptly and motioned to Kit and me. "As long as it's okay with your mother, you can come back to my house."

"But Jamie—"

"He has to go with the police," she said, walking back toward her truck.

I turned to Jamie. He was watching me, his face strained.

"I want all of us to stay together," I said again.

Jamie shook his head. "It's going to be okay, Luce. You guys go."

42

"But —"

"Go."

I touched his hand, but he wasn't looking at me. The two cops were within earshot now, listening to us, waiting. I followed Beth to the truck.

A few minutes later, Kit opened the passenger door and slid onto the seat next to me. He leaned his face close to my ear. "Don't worry," he whispered. "This is just the normal stuff they do. It doesn't mean anything."

"How do you know?" I whispered back, staring through the wet windshield at Jamie. "How do you know what stuff they do? Are they arresting him? Is he going to jail?" I could feel the tears running down my cheeks. I hoped it was too dark for Kit to see.

"No, Luce! Jeez. Cut it out."

The sheriff came to Kit's side, resting his hand on the door. "You're all set," he said. "Miss Martinez, your mother wants you to call as soon as you get to Ms. Osway's house."

I rubbed my wet cheeks and nodded, not looking at him. He slammed the door shut, and it was like a gate closing, with us on one side and Jamie on the other. The two cops were leading him toward one of their cars. As he walked away, I could see the angles of his shoulder blades jutting through his wet shirt, as thin and fragile as wings.

8

The truck jolted onto Beth's road, and a minute later we were at the house. The dogs were inside, leaping at the windows and barking in frantic bursts.

"Oh, for chrissake," Beth said. "Get your bags from the car," she said to us, then climbed out, shouting, "Settle down!"

When she opened the door, the dogs jumped all over us, thrusting their cold noses against our legs. Beth shoved them away. "No, Oscar! Toronto, down!"

Kit and I stood in the entry, not sure what to do. "I have a spare bed," Beth said to me. "You can sleep there." She turned to Kit. "I'll get some blankets for you. The study has a pretty thick rug."

Kit was staring at the half-painted metal thing in the living room. "What is that?" he asked.

"A piece I'm working on."

"Yeah? Like a sculpture?" He walked over to it and started to put his hand on one of the pipes.

"Don't touch it," Beth said. "It's still wet."

"What's it made of?"

"Metal. Car parts. Things I found."

Kit grinned. "Looks like junk," he said.

Which was exactly what I'd expect him to say. He sounded almost back to normal.

"It *is* junk," Beth replied, calmly.

Kit walked around it. "What are you going to do with it?"

"It's a commission. It'll be installed at the Albuquerque airport this fall."

"You're kidding me. Somebody's *paying* you for that?"

Beth disappeared down the hallway, calling over her shoulder, "Quite a lot of money, actually."

She came back with blankets and pillows spilling over her arms. "I know it's late, but is there anyone you should call? Your parents?"

Kit swung his duffel over his shoulder and shook his head quickly. "Mine are away. I'll try to call them tomorrow."

Suddenly, I felt an overwhelming need to hear my mom's voice, her safe, steady voice, reminding me to put sunscreen on the back of my neck and to help Jamie read the map. "I have to call my mom," I said. I thought of Jamie.

"The reception's not great here," Beth said. "Use the portable in the bedroom."

"I have a phone card," I said quickly.

She glanced at me. "Don't worry about it."

The spare bedroom was a tiny room with a double bed that took up almost all the floor space. The walls were painted dark blue, and one large bare window framed the desert night. It would be like sleeping up in the sky. Yesterday, I would have liked that, the floating freedom of it. Now I wasn't so sure.

"If you get cold," Beth said from the doorway, "there's an extra blanket under the bed."

I pushed the door partway closed while I changed. The bracelet clinked when my jacket hit the floor. I fished it out, dangling it in the light. But then I heard Kit in the hallway, so I quickly slipped it into the pocket of my backpack and dug out the phone card instead.

Would Jamie have talked to our mom by now? From the police station? I shuddered, thinking of him in a cell. Alone. I wondered what he'd told her. At home, whenever he ratted on me for something, he'd give up everything, each incriminating detail doled out with perfect timing, to maximize her outrage. I usually did the same thing to him. But this was different. Whatever it was, we were in it together. I thought of when we were little, when we broke the gutter jumping off the garage roof, or when we stuck a deck of playing cards in the fan to make confetti. I was pretty sure he'd tell our mom a short version, just enough for her to make sense of it.

But who could really make sense of it?

I cracked the window, and a cold shaft of air blew over me. Shivering, I crawled under the covers and lifted the phone from its cradle next to the bed, punching in numbers, following the string of tinny instructions.

"Hello?" She picked up on the first ring.

I pulled the phone under the blanket and pressed it against my face. "Mom?"

"Lucy! Lucy."

Her voice was ragged with worry. As soon as I heard it, I could feel years collapsing. I tried to talk, but the words caught in my throat. "Mom…"

"Oh, honey."

I could see the exact look on her face, the crumpling mix of love and fear that always made me feel so much worse than whatever it was I'd done to myself. I couldn't stand it.

I scrunched my eyes shut and tried to make my voice normal. "It's okay, Mom. Everything's okay."

"Lucy," she said. "I can't believe this happened!"

"I know. But don't worry. We're all fine."

"How's Jamie? I just talked to him and he seemed… He didn't sound like himself. And where *are* you? Some stranger's house? I don't like this. I don't like it at all."

I thought about Beth. "It's safe," I said. "The police know her. She lives near the highway and it was the first house we came to, where we went after the accident. She's … she's trying to help us."

47

I heard the sound of tires in the yard, and an orange light danced across the wall of the room. The dogs started barking again. There were voices, Beth's and someone else's, low and blending.

"What's that?" my mom asked sharply. "What's that noise?"

"The tow truck," I said. "They're taking our car."

My mom sighed. "I just can't believe you're down there on your own. You shouldn't be by yourselves, dealing with this." She was quiet for a minute, then her voice was firm. "I'll call your father. He'll come get you. He just has to."

I didn't say anything. I knew that wouldn't happen.

"Lucy, have you talked to him?"

"No, but I will, Mom."

"Okay, honey. Well, it's late. You should go to sleep. You must be exhausted."

"Yeah." I didn't want to hang up. "Mom?"

"What, honey?"

I couldn't stop thinking about the girl. I wanted to tell her about the girl's wide, staring eyes, about the way her arm arced over her head. But I thought of my mom alone in her house, worrying about us, and I didn't say anything.

"Good night, honey. And Lucy?"

"Yes?" I waited, hopeful.

"This isn't on somebody else's phone bill, is it? Did you use the phone card?"

I sighed. "Yeah, I used the card."

"Good. We'll talk tomorrow, okay?"

"Okay." I tightened my fingers around the phone. "Mom?"

"What, honey?"

The silence crackled over the line, and I could feel myself beating uselessly against it, like a moth in a jar.

"Mom, do you think you could ... could you stay on the phone for a while?"

I heard her rustling out of bed, moving into the kitchen. Her voice got louder and closer as she pressed the phone against her shoulder. "Sure, honey. I can't sleep anyway. You try to relax. I'll pay some bills."

I curled on my side and switched off the light. In the darkness, I listened to the soft sounds of her tearing envelopes and shuffling papers, the distant scratching of her pen. After a while, she said, "Lucy?"

"Yes?"

"Are you okay now? I don't want you to use up the whole phone card. Can you sleep?"

"I guess."

"I'll talk to you tomorrow, honey. Okay?"

"Okay. Bye."

I slid my arm out from the warm cave of the covers and set the phone back in its cradle. The window seemed too close and too big, filling the room with whatever was outside. I stared into the blackness, thinking about the girl. Maybe she was out there somewhere, floating around in that cold, planetary silence.

9

I woke up in the dark, shaking. There was someone in the room with me.

I grabbed the sheets against my chest and then saw it was the dog – the black one, Oscar. He'd nudged the door open and was standing there watching me, his tongue hanging out in an easy pant. He clicked across the floor and jumped onto the bed, flopping noisily next to my face. His breath pulsed over me, warm and stale. I put one hand on his head and stroked the silky fur between his ears, slowly, until my heart stopped racing.

I'd been dreaming about her. In the dream, we were driving through rain, that terrible rain, but we saw her this time. She was right in front of us, and Jamie tried to brake. She stretched out her arms. Her eyes were huge and frightened, and she was saying something. In the dream, we braked forever. But we hit her anyway.

I lay there petting the dog until he fell asleep. The sky outside the window began to lighten. Quietly, I climbed out of bed and unzipped the pocket of my backpack. I found the charm bracelet and hooked a finger around it, lifting it up to the window. It gleamed in the thready pink light.

I hadn't had a chance to really look at it before. There were four silver charms: a heart like the one on my bracelet at home, an hourglass, a horseshoe, and a treasure chest. When I flicked the treasure chest with my finger, the lid opened, and there were tiny glittering jewels inside – just colored glass, but pretty: red, green, purple. I thought of the girl choosing it from a rack in a store, liking the surprise of it.

Between the hourglass and the horseshoe was a link hanging down empty. I felt around the pocket of my jacket and my backpack to see if the other charm had fallen off. But I couldn't find it. Maybe it was back on the road somewhere.

I looked out at the desert, which was grayish-pink in the early light and rough with shrubs and rocks. The creased red slopes of the mountains rose in the distance. It was too early to get up. The whole house was quiet. I took the phone from the cradle and punched in the code from the phone card, then Ginny's number. Was it an hour later back home? I couldn't remember.

"Hello?" Her voice was husky and muffled. Maybe it wasn't an hour later. "Who is this?"

"Me. It's me." I whispered back. The dog flicked his ears and raised his head, watching me.

"Lucy? Jeez." I could hear her stirring under the sheets. "Where are you?"

"New Mexico. We had an accident."

"What?" She sounded more awake. "What happened? A *car* accident?"

"Yeah, a car accident." I told her quickly, still whispering. I told her about the beer and the rain and the girl lying next to the road. It seemed real suddenly, all of it, as if the words were pinning it down and making it something you could stand back and look at.

When I stopped talking, Ginny was quiet. "Holy shit," she said finally.

That was why I'd called her. She always said exactly what I felt.

"What are you going to *do*?"

"Jamie's at the police station. They have to check the car, and, I don't know, other stuff."

"But what's going to happen to you guys? I mean, to Jamie? He was the one driving."

"I don't know." I thought of Jamie and that smile he used on everybody: Maddie Dilworth, Kristi Bendall, the waitresses at the diners. It seemed so long ago.

Ginny exhaled into the phone, a long whoosh of breath. "Is he in *jail*? I mean, did they arrest him?"

I flinched. "No! No. Don't say that. It wasn't his fault."

"Okay, okay."

"It was an accident."

"I know. I'm just thinking."

"It was Kit who bought the beer."

She groaned. "Kit the zit."

I heard footsteps in the hall. "I've got to go," I whispered quickly, snatching the bracelet from the nest of blankets.

"Okay, call me later."

"I will," I promised. I dropped the bracelet in my backpack just as Beth pushed open the door.

"You're up," she said. "I was looking for Oscar." She snapped her fingers and he bounded off the bed, tail wagging. "I thought he'd end up with you. He considers this his bedroom. I should've told you to latch the door."

"That's okay," I said. "I like dogs."

She turned away. "Do you? I don't. But I've gotten used to these guys."

I pulled on a pair of jeans and followed her into the kitchen. It was a long white rectangle at the back of the house: white cupboards, white tile, white wooden table at one end. There was a chipped red bowl of bananas on the counter, the only color in the room except for the window's pale square of sky.

The desert looked different now, sparkling with colors. I could see tiny clumps of yellow flowers, a cluster of lavender buds. "Hey," I said. "Look."

Beth smiled. "The desert after a storm. Everything grows at once. Flowers shoot up and bloom in a day, and you see insects and animals you never knew lived here. All because of the rain."

"How long does it last?"

"Not long. We've had hot weather lately, much hotter than usual. Everything will die back to nothing. But water does amazing things in a place as dry as this."

The phone rang, a long, shattering *brrrring*. Beth lifted the receiver from the wall.

"Hello? Oh, hi, Stan. You're at work early. Yeah, she's right here. He's still sleeping. Oh, okay. That's no problem. Around ten o'clock? Okay. What? No, I don't think so. Why don't you ask Lucy?" She handed me the phone.

I swallowed, suddenly nervous. Now what? "Hello?"

"Miss Martinez? This is Sheriff Durrell. I just wanted to check on something. Last night, none of you kids happened to take anything off the person of the victim, did you?"

He knew about the bracelet. But how could he?

I twisted one hand in my T-shirt and turned away so Beth wouldn't see my face. "Um," I said, trying to keep my voice ordinary. "What do you mean?"

"Well, from what your brother Jamie and the other boy ..." he paused, "Freder—"

"Kit," I said.

"Right, Kit. From what they said, none of you moved the victim."

"No, we didn't do anything to her," I said quickly. "I mean, I pulled down her shirt because it was up over her stomach, but—"

"The reason I ask is that we're not finding any ID on her. No wallet, no license, no purse or other kind of personal effects. It's – well, it's unusual, and it's going to make our job a lot harder. I wondered if you or the boys might have picked something up at the scene. Something that belonged to the victim." He hesitated. "I understand you were pretty upset, and maybe you didn't realize..." He was waiting for me to say something.

But I couldn't do it. He wasn't looking for a bracelet, anyway. He was looking for something with her name on it. The bracelet didn't matter to anyone but me. "No," I said. "That's how she was when we found her."

"Hmmm. Well, okay, then. We've examined the car, and we should have the preliminary coroner's report in a few hours. I told Ms. Osway that I'm going to release your brother for the time being."

"You are?" I gripped the phone, my stomach fluttering with hope. "It's all right for him to leave?"

"Not leave the area, no. But his alcohol level and everything else checked out okay. We don't need to keep him here at the station, as long as I know where to reach him." He paused. "I'll see you later today, Miss Martinez."

"Okay. Bye." I hung up the phone and turned to Beth, who was watching me. "He said Jamie can go."

She nodded. "Yes, we can pick him up around ten. That's good. I guess the Breathalyzer test turned out fine."

"So they know it wasn't his fault? They won't, like, press charges or anything?"

She poured coffee into two mugs. "He didn't say that," she said carefully.

"But don't you think—"

"I think it's good that they're releasing him." She looked at me with the same appraising gaze she seemed to wear, not sympathetic, not even polite, just watchful and assessing. "But I wouldn't assume anything. Not when someone's dead."

I flinched.

She pushed one of the mugs across the counter toward me and cupped hers with both hands. She was silent. I sniffed the bitter steam. It reminded me of my mom having breakfast at home. I didn't usually drink coffee, but now I tasted it, somehow afraid not to. It scalded my tongue.

I tried to think of something else to talk about. "How long have you lived here?"

"Nine years. I came from Detroit."

"Really? By yourself? You don't have a husband or kids or anything?"

"No. I'm divorced. He took the house, I got the dogs."

"But you said you don't like dogs."

"Right. That's divorce. You each get half, but not the half you want." She smiled a little, running her hands through her hair and tucking it behind her ears. "I'm used to them now."

I thought of how this place seemed at night, as vast and bottomless as the ocean. I couldn't imagine living here by myself. "Aren't you scared? Being out here alone?"

Beth sipped her coffee. "No, not really. The dogs are too friendly to be much protection, but they make a lot of noise." She looked out the window. "I like it here. It's quiet. And when you get used to it, the desert's beautiful."

"But it's so empty," I said.

Beth nodded. "It is empty. But it changes in little ways, all the time. And it's not … distracting, like so many other places are."

I thought about my town in Kansas, a few miles from Kansas City. It didn't seem distracting. Just inhabited. Roads, houses, stores, farms, the cross-hatching of people's lives. I missed it, the way everything was connected to something else.

I put my mug in the sink. "I'm going to see if Kit's awake."

He and Jamie would sleep till noon if nobody woke them. I tried each of the closed doors along the hallway – two closets, a bedroom, a bathroom – before I found the study, where Kit was stretched across a lumpy knot of blankets on the floor. He lay flat on his back, his hair curling over his forehead and his mouth loose and full. If you didn't know Kit, you would think he was cute. It was his personality that ruined things.

"Hey," I said into the silence. "Hey! Wake up." I nudged him with my foot. He rolled over.

"Kit," I said. "Wake up. We're going to get Jamie soon." Not soon, actually. More like two hours from now, but he didn't need to know that. I was tired of talking to Beth by myself. "The police are letting him come back here."

Kit's eyes opened. He rose up on one elbow, rubbing his hand over his hair. "They are? What happened?" He looked at his watch, then burrowed back into the pillow. "Whoa, it's early."

I pushed at him again with my foot. "You need to get up."

"Quit kicking me."

"Come on. Don't you want to get Jamie?"

"Yeah, yeah, sure," he mumbled. "But jeez, do we have to go now?"

"Soon," I said again. "Come on, Beth made coffee."

For some reason he didn't ask any more questions. He sat up and stretched, throwing his arms out in a big, exaggerated way, like somebody coming out of hibernation. He pulled his T-shirt off in one quick motion, and when I blinked and backed away, trying not to look at him, I could feel him smiling.

10

The police station was half an hour away, toward Albuquerque. I was glad we didn't have to drive by the place where we found the girl. But I wasn't sure I'd even have recognized it. The landscape looked different in the daylight, not as threatening. The dirt was salmon colored, scattered with little shrubs and feathery grasses. Beth drove fast, way above the speed limit, one hand resting lightly on the wheel. Kit kept looking at the speedometer, impressed. He tried to talk to her a couple of times but she barely answered him.

"So you kind of know those cops, huh?" he said at one point.

"What do you mean?"

"Well, it seemed like you were friends with them."

"It's a small community. Everybody knows everybody."

"But the sheriff, it seemed like he—"

"We went out for a while."

"Oh," Kit looked at her, interested. *"Oh."*

I poked him, but he just grinned, satisfied. Beth didn't say anything. We were in a town suddenly, or what must pass for a town in a place like this. There was a low assemblage of buildings, a couple of gas stations, a grocery store. The police station was a dull-looking white building close to the road.

"Just wait here," Beth said, slamming the door and striding across the parking lot.

"Look. You made her mad," I said to Kit. "Why were you asking her all those questions?"

"I knew there was something between her and that cop," Kit said. "I always pick up on that kind of thing."

"Oh, yeah, you're so perceptive," I said, rolling my eyes.

"I am," he said. "At least about that."

When Jamie came through the doors with Beth, my heart clutched. There he was in his wrinkled T-shirt from last night. His hair was clumped and tangled the way it always was first thing in the morning. But he looked different. His shoulders were hunched. His eyes were too bright.

"Hey," he said, climbing in on Beth's side. "Hey, you guys." The truck had a wide cab, but not wide enough for four. I was squashed between Jamie and Kit, their shoulders pressing hard against me.

I grabbed his arm and held it. "Are you okay? Jamie? What happened?"

60

He didn't look at me. "I'm okay."

"But what did they do to you? Were you in a cell?"

He frowned, staring through the windshield.

"What is it?" I tried to get him to look at me, but he wouldn't.

"Nothing. I just ... I'm just tired. I didn't get much sleep."

"But did they—"

"I don't want to talk about it, okay?"

I watched his face. "Okay."

He was quiet for a minute. He kept glancing at Beth, and the tight, worried look on his face suddenly shifted. I could see him trying to shake off the strangeness that had settled over him, trying to force his old self back into place. He arched his back a little, stretching, and said to Beth, "You ever give this many people a ride before?"

"No," Beth said. "It's pretty tight."

"This will make more room." Jamie lifted one arm and settled it along the seat behind Beth's shoulders.

Beth looked at him but didn't say anything.

I couldn't believe it. For a minute I thought I was wrong. But no, the expression on his face, the way his hand dangled close to her arm. What was she, twenty years older than he was? And hadn't he just been arrested for murder? Or whatever it was they'd done with him? But here he was, hitting on a woman almost our mother's age. I dug my elbow into his side.

"Ow! Hey! What'd you do that for?" he gasped.

"Sorry," I mumbled. "I was just trying to make more room." Next to me, I heard Kit stifle a laugh.

When we got back to Beth's, she drifted away from us, preoccupied. "I have to work," she said. "Help yourselves to whatever you need."

She twisted her hair into a thick rope and wound it against the back of her head. Then she stuck a pen through it, holding it in place.

"How'd you do that?" Jamie asked, watching her.

"Lots of practice."

He smiled at her. "You have great hair."

Beth's brow twitched and she looked at him curiously. "Thanks."

"Jamie," I said, trying to get his attention. "We should call Dad."

He hesitated. "Yeah. Maybe you could do it? Tell him we probably won't get there tonight."

I went back to the bedroom, and as soon as I opened the door, the dogs came pouring out, snuffling and whining. They raced toward the living room, and I heard Beth yell at them. I sat on the edge of the bed, dialing my dad's work number. He wouldn't be in his office; he almost never was. He was a sales rep for an insurance company, and he spent half his time on the road.

I listened to the four short beeps of his answering machine, then the impersonal friendliness of his work voice: "This is Bob Martinez. I'm away from my desk right now, but leave me a message and I'll return your call as soon as possible."

I took a deep breath. "Dad? It's me, Lucy. We're calling from New Mexico, some place outside Albuquerque. We..." I tried to think how to say it. "We had kind of an accident, you know, with the car. Nobody's hurt—" I took another breath. "Well, we're not hurt, but we think we hit somebody, a girl, and she's—" I scrunched the hem of my T-shirt and pressed it against my stomach. "We don't really know what happened. It was raining so hard, we couldn't see. But she's dead. The girl is dead. So now we're here and we've been talking to the police. And Mom said, well, Mom wondered if maybe you could come..."

As soon as I said it I wished I hadn't. I didn't want to ask and hear him say no, even though the reason would be a good one, and when he explained, it would make so much more sense for him to stay in Phoenix and for us to work things out on our own. I held the phone closer. "But, um, probably you don't need to do that. I mean, we're at this woman's house and things are sort of under control now. But we won't get to Phoenix tonight. We have to stay until—" A long, sullen tone cut me off. The machine clicked.

I carried the phone back into the living room, which was filled with the smell of fresh paint. Beth knelt on the speckled drop cloth, her face tense with concentration. She had a brush in one hand and was dabbing the bottom of the sculpture with turquoise.

"That's pretty," I said. "That color."

She didn't look up. Jamie and Kit were sprawled on the couch, watching her.

"Did you get him?" Jamie asked.

I shook my head. "I left him a message."

"That's okay. We can try him again later."

I held out the phone to Kit. "Want to call your parents now?"

Kit kicked at a pile of newspapers. "Maybe later."

I walked past them and sat on the floor, next to the wild twist of metal at the base of the sculpture. It was hard to figure out what it was made of, but when I looked closely, I could see a tailpipe, two dented license plates, and something that looked like a barbecue grill.

"When do you think we'll get our car back?" I asked.

Jamie frowned. "When they get the lab results, I guess."

"Are they…" I swallowed. "Did they say anything about the beer? They aren't going to … arrest you or anything?"

Kit blew out his breath hard. "God, you're so negative." He turned to Jamie. "I can see why you didn't want to drive the whole way with her by yourself."

I looked at Jamie, stung. But he was ignoring us, watching Beth paint.

"So why do you use car parts and pipes and stuff?" he asked.

She moved the paintbrush over the steel with bold strokes. "I like using things people get rid of," she said.

64

Kit trapped a sheet of newspaper under one foot and slid it back and forth on the floor. "How come? I mean, I've seen things like this before, made out of metal. You could get a piece of stainless steel, brand new, and really do something cool with it. None of this crap with old license plates."

Jamie smacked his shoulder. "Shut up."

"Hey," Kit said, rubbing it. "I was just asking."

Beth sat back on her heels and balanced the paintbrush between her thumb and forefinger. She looked from Kit to Jamie. "That's all right. People are entitled to their opinions. This isn't for everyone."

"What is it?" I asked. "What's it called?"

"Joshua Tree. I do natural forms. That's the point. Nature out of machines."

I could see it then. The twist of the trunk, the way the pieces of metal gave it a texture, roots, bark.

Jamie leaned forward, smiling at her. "I like it. It's different."

Beth shrugged. "This is just the base. I do it in pieces."

Kit cocked his head to the side. "It doesn't look like a tree."

"When I put the whole thing together, it will."

"But I still don't get it. Why do you use junk?"

Beth considered him for a minute. I knew she was trying to decide whether it was worth having this conversation. I felt like warning her that it wasn't.

She went back to painting. It was hypnotizing to watch.

Her hand was so steady, so sure of what it was doing. I leaned my head against the sofa.

"It's pretty abstract," she said. "A way of seeing things." She hesitated. "There's so much ugliness around, you know? What you see on the highways, on city sidewalks, shoved behind people's garages. All the junk. Nothing in nature is like that. Nothing is ugly like that."

Kit looked at Jamie. "She hasn't seen Lisa Becker," he said.

I hit his leg with my fist. "Shut up, Kit."

He turned on me, annoyed. "What? She's not a friend of yours."

Beth just shook her head, giving up. But Jamie was still watching her. "Go on," he said. "Finish what you were saying."

She sighed. "I don't know. It's hard to explain. Since I started doing this, it's changed the way I look at things. Now, when I notice a smashed can on the side of the road, I don't see somebody's trash, I see the potential for…" she paused.

"A sculpture?" Jamie asked.

"Well, yes. Art." Beth smiled at him, a widening smile that lit up her whole face. "If you look at the most ordinary thing long enough, it can seem beautiful."

"Huh," Kit said. He seemed unimpressed. "And people pay you for this stuff? You make a living doing this?"

"Well, sort of. I teach art classes for half the year."

"Yeah?" Jamie leaned forward. "You teach? I bet you're good at that."

Beth looked at him. "Why?"

I watched him, thinking how goofy it was. He was using his same old moves on this middle-aged woman who couldn't care less.

"I just mean, you're so good at painting and all, I think you'd be good at explaining it to people."

She shrugged. "They're two different skills. I'm not as good at the teaching as I am at the painting. I don't really like having to deal with people."

Jamie and Kit and I looked at each other. That shut us up.

11

After a while, Jamie said, "Could I take a shower? I feel pretty gross from last night."

"Of course. There are fresh towels in the bathroom closet."

Kit and I stayed there in silence, watching the sculpture change with the paint. Finally, the distant whine of the shower stopped and Jamie called, "Did you guys get my bag from the car last night?"

"Yeah, it's in the study," Kit said. He got up and wandered down the hall. After a minute, I followed him.

Jamie came out of the study toweling off his hair. "Is Beth still painting?" he asked.

The expression on his face was completely familiar, a kind of eager alertness, exactly how he looked when he and Kit were talking about some girl he liked.

"Jamie, she's got to be in her thirties," I whispered, appalled.

He looked annoyed. "What are you talking about?"

"I'm talking about you hitting on Beth, you moron. What are you doing, talking and talking to her? And you tried to put your arm around her in the truck."

"I did not!"

Kit laughed. "So what if he did? She's sort of hot. She's got the older-woman thing going."

They were incredible. It was one thing at the diners and the gas stops. We were never going to see those people again. But we were in this woman's house. "She's got gray hair," I said, gasping.

Kit considered that for a minute, then shrugged at Jamie. "Yeah," he said. "She could be kind of saggy. And she was a bitch about the beer."

Jamie balled the damp towel in his fist. "Back off, Luce. What's it to you, anyway? I'm not hitting on her. I just like her, that's all."

I turned away. "When have you ever liked somebody and not hit on them?"

"Oh, give me a break."

Kit laughed again, grabbing my shoulder and shoving me down the hallway. "Yeah, give him a break. You're too young to understand."

That made me so mad I stopped talking to them. But they didn't seem to notice. They headed into the kitchen and Jamie called to Beth, "Hey, can you take a break?

Want some coffee?"

"Does that mean you want me to make you coffee?" Beth called back.

Jamie laughed. "Yeah. Do you mind?"

And amazingly, she didn't. She rinsed her hands at the kitchen sink, and Jamie and Kit immediately went into high gear, both of them. They were grinning and chatting, complimenting her on the sculpture, the house, the coffee. It was crazy. How could they do this when we were in so much trouble? How could they turn that part of themselves back on, like a switch, when a girl had died?

Beth seemed to wonder the same thing, because as she poured their coffee, she said, "The police are going to call later. Did Lucy tell you? When they're finished with the car."

Jamie winced, nodding. Kit looked at the table.

"That girl," she continued, "she wasn't much older than you. But there's something really strange about it. She was miles from anywhere, and nobody walks along the highway out here. I wonder where she came from."

"She wasn't banged up, either," Kit said. "Like, wouldn't you expect that, from the car?"

Jamie frowned at him, starting to say something, but Beth answered first. "I don't know. If she were struck and thrown, the injuries could be mostly internal."

We were quiet, thinking about her. Where had she come from? Maybe somebody woke up this morning, missing her, worried about her. They didn't realize she wasn't coming back.

"Sit down," Jamie said to Beth, pulling a chair away from the table.

Beth shook her head. "I'm going back to work."

"Come on. Sit with us." He called the brown dog, Toronto, over to him, ruffling her ears while she leaned against his leg.

Beth hesitated, but Kit refilled her mug, saying, "Oh, come on, what are you going to do, stick another hubcap on that thing?"

Shouldn't she be offended by that? I mean, he was talking about her work, her art. But for some reason it made her laugh. And when she laughed, she seemed even prettier.

Beth looked from Kit to Jamie and asked, "Have you been friends a long time?"

Jamie took her arm, smiling at her, and tugged her down to the chair, so she was crowded between them. Then they began telling their stories. Their you'll-never-believe-what-we-did stories. I'd heard them all: the practical jokes and close calls and times when they said the perfect, hilarious thing at exactly the right moment. It was too intense suddenly. Like they usually were, but more of it. This was a performance.

I could feel myself disappearing, bit by bit, fading into the room. So I left. I went back to the bedroom and got my sketchbook. Then I sat in the hallway near the door, listening to them talk. I didn't know what to sketch, but I drew quick lines on the page, and after a minute, I realized I was drawing her face. The girl's.

In the kitchen, Jamie was saying, "Digger – he's the principal, Mr. DiGennaro – is a total hard-ass. He canceled the senior chorus trip to Chicago last December because three guys on the chorus council were caught drinking—"

Kit snorted. "Yeah, *after* school, and in their own cars. That was totally bogus."

Beth looked confused. "Wait, you two are in chorus?"

They both laughed. "No way," Kit said. "They're all losers. But we can't stand Digger."

"Yeah," said Jamie, leaning forward. "So, listen, Digger'd just gotten this new car, an Acura, nice car, he was totally into it—"

Kit interrupted, "And there was a faculty meeting before school, so we got there early, and we brought, like, four bags of Oreos—"

Jamie started laughing. "And right there in the parking lot, we Oreo-ed his entire car. You know, pulled the Oreos apart and stuck them all over his windows. It was so great. The whole top half of his car was black."

I heard Beth's voice lift in amazement. "The principal's car? And you didn't get caught?"

"That was nothing," Kit said.

I glanced through the doorway and watched them, that weird choreography they had, feeding each other lines, finishing each other's sentences, playing to Beth as if she were the only person in the world. She was laughing, but I couldn't tell whether it was at the stories or at Jamie and Kit.

Jamie grinned at Kit. "Remember the toilets in the teachers' lounge?"

Kit tilted back his chair and whistled. "Oh my God, that was so great. That was magnificent."

"What?" Beth asked, still laughing. "What did you do?"

Jamie leaned closer to her. "You're going to love this. We snuck into the teachers' lounge before school and put clingfilm under the toilet seats, between the seat and the bowl. We stretched it so tight it was completely clear."

"No," Beth protested, her hand over her mouth.

Jamie was cracking up. "You couldn't see it at all. Remember, Kit? Mrs. Bottner got so pissed."

"Yeah, pissed *on,* " Kit said.

I couldn't believe they were telling her this, or that she was finding it funny.

I'd always thought flirting was something obvious, like those things people said in movies, with raised eyebrows and long sexy stares. But with Kit and Jamie, it was different, a way of paying attention to someone, turning a normal conversation into a private spark of connection.

Toronto scrambled to her feet, ears pricked. I stood up and looked out the kitchen window. "Hey," I said.

They all stopped talking and turned toward me. I pointed. A police car was rolling toward the house, its hood flashing in the sunlight.

12

The sudden silence in the kitchen was strange after their noisy stream of conversation. Jamie's face lost all expression. He stared at the floor.

Beth stood up. "I wonder what they want."

The dogs started barking and bounded past us toward the entryway. Beth hauled them back by their collars. She swore at them, herding them into the room where I'd slept.

Sheriff Durrell stood on the porch. His metallic sunglasses hid his eyes. All I could see when I looked at him was my own distorted reflection: a wide, wavy face over a tiny, diminishing body.

"Hello, folks," he said. "Can I talk to you for a few minutes?"

Jamie nodded, quiet now, and we stepped blinking, barefoot, into the yard. The sun was high and the red sand glared back at us, brassy and unforgiving.

"We took samples from your car," the sheriff said. "We should have results in a couple of hours. The rain washed it down pretty good, but we got something off the bumper."

What was it? What did he find? I could feel a shift in the air, a friction that hadn't been there before.

He was looking at Jamie. "I want you to tell me again what you saw. Where the impact was."

He led Jamie away from us. All I could hear was a muffled exchange, no words. Beth stood next to me, fiddling with the pen in her hair.

When they came back, Jamie's face looked pinched.

"You won't be going anywhere. Understand?" the sheriff said. He turned to Beth. "They'll need to make other arrangements for a place to stay."

Beth was watching Jamie. "It's okay," she said finally. "They can stay here for another night or two. It doesn't matter."

"Thanks," Jamie said softly.

The sheriff frowned. I wondered what he was thinking. That we'd try to take off? Nobody knew us here.

"All right," he said. "I'll be in touch later this afternoon."

As the sheriff drove away, Kit shielded his eyes with his hand and watched. I thought of the beer cans scattered in the brush somewhere. I wondered if you could see them from the road.

"Man, it's hot," Kit said. "Jamie, you want to go out for a while? Get some lunch?"

Jamie nodded. "Sure, but we don't have a car."

Beth glanced at him, then shrugged. "You can take the truck, I guess."

Jamie grinned. "Really? Thanks. Is there a restaurant around here?"

"Yeah, about ten miles west, on the left."

I climbed the porch stairs, brushing off the soles of my feet. "I have to get my sandals."

Kit looked at Jamie, making a face that he thought I couldn't see, but of course I could. "Uh ... why don't you just hang out here," he said to me. "We'll bring you something."

My cheeks were hot. I felt stupid. "Okay," I said quickly. "Get me a turkey sandwich."

Jamie seemed not to notice. "Beth? You want anything?"

She shook her head, tossing Jamie the keys. "Drive carefully."

Inside, Beth went back to painting and I rested my chin on the back of the couch, watching them leave. I could see the two of them laughing in the cab of the truck.

"Do you want a soda?" Beth asked.

She was trying to be nice. But I was embarrassed that she'd seen how they treated me. "No, I'm okay," I said.

I got my sketch pad from the hallway and propped it

against my knees, looking at the drawing of the girl. I'd finished her hair and her neck, the shape of her face. I started to work on her eyes.

"You like to draw?" Beth asked, after a while.

I nodded.

"What kinds of things?"

I shrugged. "Animals, people. Sometimes places."

"What's your favorite thing to draw?"

I thought for a minute. "Faces, I guess."

"Yeah?" Beth set down her brush, wiping her hands on a towel. "Show me something you've done."

She came toward the couch and I flipped the pages backward, quickly. I didn't want her to see the girl. I found a picture I'd drawn of my mom reading. "Here," I said, turning it for her to see.

She took it from me. I felt nervous suddenly. Everybody always said I was good at drawing: my parents, my art teachers, everybody. It didn't matter what Beth thought. But it did somehow. I waited.

"It's good," she said. "Technically very good. The shadows, the proportions."

I relaxed. "Thanks."

"Who is it?"

"My mom."

"Hmmm." She tilted her head, still looking at the sketch.

"What?" I started to take it back.

"Nothing. It's good, but I wouldn't have known it was your mom."

"Well, how could you?" I said, settling it back on my knees. "You've never met her."

Beth picked up her brush and knelt by the sculpture again. "No. But that's the next step. Drawing what you feel, not just what you see."

I didn't say anything. I didn't know what she meant, but it sounded like she didn't think I was that great at drawing after all.

Beth started painting again. "If you draw what you feel," she said, "anyone who sees that sketch should be able to tell it's your mom. You know?"

I stared at the paper. "I guess."

I flipped the pages back to the drawing of the girl and started sketching her lips, slightly open, glistening the way they did in the rain. The room was quiet again. The late-afternoon sun warmed my shoulders.

Jamie and Kit were taking forever. "How far is that restaurant?" I asked.

Beth pursed her lips, shooting a quick glance out the window. "They've been gone awhile, haven't they?"

I wondered if she was worried about her truck. She dipped the paintbrush and wiped it deftly on the edge of the can. "Your brother and Kit don't seem very much alike. How long have they been friends?"

"A long time. Since third grade."

Too long, I wanted to say. I thought about the two of them having lunch. I knew exactly what they were doing. Those hours in the car, listening to them talk about girls, then sitting by myself at the restaurants. I was mad at them all over again. I thought about Kit making fun of me, making me stay here while they went out to lunch. Then I remembered the look on Jamie's face: that intense, eager look whenever he caught Beth's attention or made her smile.

Suddenly, I knew exactly what to say next.

"Yeah, they've been friends for a long time, but they've only been, you know, a *couple,* since last year."

13

Beth stopped painting. "What?"

I couldn't look at her. I kept my eyes on my sketch pad. "You know," I said again. "They're, like, together."

I could feel her staring at me. "They're *together*? You mean they're gay?"

I looked at her quickly. She was standing in front of the sculpture, dangling the paintbrush, her face full of surprise. "Wow. I didn't get that from them at all."

I ran one finger along the windowsill, leaving a thin streak through the dust. "Well, they're pretty private about it."

"Is that why they wanted to go to lunch by themselves?" she asked.

I hadn't even thought of that, but now I nodded firmly. "I guess they wanted a little time alone." It was almost hard not to laugh.

"Huh," Beth said. She swirled the paintbrush in the can at her feet. "I'm just … I'm really surprised. I'm usually pretty good at picking up the signals. Jamie – actually, both of them – well, whatever." She went back to painting, but then stopped again. "That must be hard for them, being in high school. And in Kansas, too."

I could feel myself losing control of the story. I was never good at lying. And for some reason – even though they were such jerks, even though this was the perfect way to stop whatever might be happening between Jamie and Beth – I felt a stab of guilt.

"They're not really out yet," I said. "So they probably wouldn't want you to know."

"Oh. Okay."

Just then the phone rang. Beth motioned with the paintbrush, so I picked it up. "Hello?"

"Beth?"

"No. Would you like to talk to her?"

"Oh. Is this Miss Martinez?"

Now I recognized the voice. "Yes," I said warily.

"Sheriff Durrell here. I've got some good news for you and your brother, Miss Martinez. We just got the preliminary report from the coroner's office. We have an estimated time of death for the victim."

I looked down at my sketch, at her quiet, staring face. How was that good news? "Oh," I said.

"It's two p.m."

I didn't understand. "But it was at night," I said. "It was dark when we hit her."

"We don't think you hit her, Miss Martinez. We think that girl died five, six hours earlier."

I leaned forward slowly, holding the phone so tightly I thought it would break in my hand. "What?"

Beth put down her paintbrush. "What is it? Lucy, what's the matter?"

The sheriff kept talking. "Those samples we took from the car. There was some kind of animal fur on the license plate."

"You mean ... Jamie was right? It was a coyote?" I couldn't believe it. I was tingly and numb at the same time, as if something heavy was sliding off my body and the feeling was rushing back into my arms and legs all at once.

"Lucy, who are you talking to?" Beth came and stood next to me. I was gripping the phone, straining to hear his answer.

"Well, that's what we think. Your brother said you didn't know the exact spot where you hit whatever you hit. Maybe when you drove back, you went too far, or not far enough. And you found her instead."

I could breathe now, huge gulps of air. But it still didn't make sense. "But she was near the road. If she'd been there all afternoon, in the daylight, wouldn't somebody else have seen her?"

"Well, two o'clock was the time of death. We don't know what time she was left there."

When he said that – "left there" – I realized what it meant. Somebody had done this to her. Somebody had left her there, dead, on the highway.

"We'll drop off the car in a little while," he said. "Okay, Miss Martinez? Can you put Beth on for a minute?"

I passed the phone to her and covered my face with my hands.

"What a relief," I heard her say. "Jamie especially – well, they'll be so relieved, I know. But how did she die? Yes, I understand. It's terrible." I spread my fingers, watching her, and she listened in silence, looking back at me. "They've talked to their parents. Sure. I think so. Yes, I think you're right. That's good of you, Stan. Thank you. Okay. Bye."

She reached out and touched my arm. "Lucy, he's giving you guys a break on the beer."

I pressed my forehead against my knees, closing my eyes. Was it really over? "Then we can go? Is it okay for us to go now?"

But I wasn't sure even as I said it. I kept seeing the girl's face, feeling the cool bundle of her charm bracelet in my hand. It seemed wrong to leave her. It seemed as wrong to leave her now as it had last night, in the rain, on the road.

Beth shook her head. "Not yet. He wants you to stay through tomorrow, at least."

The dogs started barking out in the yard, and we heard

the sound of the truck rumbling toward the house. Jamie and Kit were back.

We both got up, and the instant they walked through the door, I couldn't wait, I forgot what jerks they'd been and how mad I was, and I grabbed the first one who came in and wrapped my arms around him. It was Kit, and his shoulder felt warm against my face. Then he stumbled backward, his hands on my arms. He looked confused. "Hey, what's going on?"

But I was already hugging Jamie. "The police called. It wasn't us!"

"What?" They were both staring at me.

"We didn't hit her. She was already dead, hours before we even got there. They think it was a coyote! They think we hit a coyote." The words came out of my mouth in a rush, tumbling over each other. Kit and Jamie just stood there.

But then Beth started explaining, and Kit threw his head back and whistled, long and low. "No way. No *way*. It *was* a coyote!" He punched Jamie's shoulder. "Jamie, it was a coyote, just like you said! Oh my God." Kit grabbed Jamie and lifted him right off the floor.

Beth stepped aside, smiling. "And Stan – the sheriff is letting you off the hook on the drinking," she said. "He said this was probably the scare of a lifetime for you guys."

"Yeah!" Kit was reeling around, flushed and loud, banging the air with his fist. "Yeah, yeah, no kidding. Unbelievable."

But Jamie just stared at the floor. The color had drained from his face, and he stood there, trembling. "I can't believe it," he said. "I can't believe it's over."

Beth touched his shoulder. "Believe it," she said. "It's over."

14

The rest of the day blurred past. I couldn't eat the sandwich they'd gotten me, couldn't eat dinner that night when Beth offered it. It was weird to think of doing something normal again. The police brought our car back around sunset. We were elated to see it, our dusty old sedan. It felt like a reunion. Jamie and Kit opened the windows, apologetic in front of the cops. It still reeked of beer.

That night, we talked endlessly about the accident, every single detail of it: what we'd been doing in the car right before, what we'd said, what we'd seen. It was like we were trying to make up for the long silence that had settled over us since it happened. Finally, we could replay that scene on the highway – how the rain came, how we felt the bump, how we kept going – because this time we didn't hit her. This time it wasn't our fault.

"You jammed on the brakes, remember?" Kit said.

"No," Jamie shook his head, "there wasn't time. I braked afterwards."

"Yeah, and we skidded," I reminded them.

Now Kit thought he remembered a gray streak in front of the car. I wondered if I'd seen it, too.

Jamie called our mom, and we had to both get on the phone, one on the portable and one in the kitchen, to hear her crying, "Oh, thank God! Oh, Jamie, Lucy, I can't tell you how worried I was."

Then she asked about our dad – she'd called him, was he coming for us? – and at least we could say that he wouldn't have to now. Not that he wouldn't come, but that he wouldn't have to. We'd be driving to Phoenix in a day or so. "But that's almost halfway through your vacation," my mom protested.

"It's okay," Jamie told her. "It'll work out."

We called our dad afterward. It was late enough to call him at home, and he picked up on the first ring. As soon as he heard my voice, he said, "Lucy! Why didn't you leave a number? I've been trying the cell all afternoon, but it wouldn't go through. What the hell's going on?"

And I had to explain it again, but it was so much easier now. Plus, I could tell that my dad only cared about the ending, because he kept interrupting with questions like, "So you guys are fine? No damage to the car? When are you going to get here?"

"I think we can leave tomorrow or the next day," I told him. "The police have to go through the lab report or something."

"Give me the number for the police station. I want to talk to them directly."

So Beth got it for him, and I kept reassuring him, until finally he said, "Well, I hope you can leave tomorrow, because I've got meetings all day Wednesday and Thursday, and now the weekend's shot. Okay, babe, put your brother on."

Listening to Jamie's end of the conversation, I could tell he was getting the predictable lecture, about driving in the rain, or driving too fast, or braking when something came into the road. With my dad, it didn't matter if it wasn't your fault. There was always something you could have done differently. Jamie kept saying, "Yeah, Dad. Yeah, I know. I'll remember."

Then Kit finally called his parents. He paced around the living room, his voice too loud, piling on the details. I could feel it happening as he spoke: this terrible thing, the girl dead on the road, was turning into one of his close calls. A near miss, a disaster that wasn't. He would tell this story as proof of something. But of what? I thought about the girl. Everything had changed for us. Nothing had changed for her.

"So don't worry," Kit was saying. "Everything's fine now."

"Kit," I said quietly. "She's still dead."

* * *

That night, I curled up under the blankets and faced the window. It was like looking through the porthole of a spaceship, directly into the universe. I couldn't sleep. I'd left my door open a crack, hoping one of the dogs would come. But the house was quiet.

Then I heard something. It was a strange sound, a muffled kind of choking coming from the hallway. But the stranger thing was, I recognized it. In some buried part of my brain, I knew what it was. I sat up and listened. Slowly, as quietly as I could, I pushed back the covers and slid my feet onto the floor. I padded to the door and put my face against the crack.

Jamie was in the hallway. He was crouched against the wall, knees drawn up, head down, sitting in a long rectangle of moonlight. He was crying.

I started to open the door and go to him the way he'd done for me a long time ago, after our dad left and I used to cry at night.

Then I saw Beth.

She slipped through her bedroom doorway into the hall, wearing a thin white nightgown covered in flowers. It swirled around her like a meadow when she knelt beside him. She put her arm around his shoulders.

I heard her voice, soft and low, saying, "Jamie, what is it? What's the matter?" And then, "Shhh. I know it was scary for you. It would have been for anybody. But it's over now."

She kept talking to him. Her hair fell forward, hiding

her face, and I couldn't hear the rest. Then I saw Jamie lift his head, his cheeks wet. And I felt my stomach clutch because I knew what was about to happen. I knew it before they did.

His hand reached up to touch her hair.

Beth pulled away, and in the patch of light, I saw the stricken look on her face. "No," she said.

He took her hand and turned it over, slowly, so her palm cupped the moonlight. Then he brought it up to his mouth and kissed it.

"Jamie," she said again. "I don't understand. I thought you and Kit – I thought you were—"

But it was too late. He was pulling her forward, holding on to her like he thought she might fall, or he might. Then he was kissing her, touching her face and kissing her.

I stepped away from the door. I pushed it closed, noiselessly, and climbed back into bed.

It wasn't over.

15

When I woke up in the morning, I thought I had dreamed it. It was too strange, what happened in the hallway. It had the feel of a dream, a weird dream, coming after that weird day. The night had been long and restless. I'd dreamed about the girl again, but this time when she rose up in front of the car she was wearing a white nightgown, and it billowed out like the sail of a ship.

I untangled the sheets and blinked at the blaze of sky that filled the window. Beth was so much older than we were. Jamie was still a kid. I'd seen Jamie kiss girls before, up against the lockers at school, or leaning into somebody's car. But I'd never seen him kiss anyone like that. It couldn't have been real.

I pulled on my jeans and tiptoed into the quiet hallway. It was late, but nobody seemed to be up. Beth's door was closed. The door to the study was open a crack. I walked toward it thinking they'd be in there, Jamie and Kit, sleeping, just like Kit was yesterday. But I think I knew before I pushed it open: the only one there was Kit.

I stood looking at him, lying on his back, breathing his deep, slow breaths. I wished – just for a minute, but fiercely – that he was the one in the bedroom with Beth and that Jamie was here, safe.

Suddenly, I had to get out of the house. It was too much, the car accident, the dead girl, and now Jamie sleeping with a woman twenty years older than he was. It felt like we'd left Kansas and stepped into some upside-down world where there were no rules.

I ran down the hallway, my feet skimming over the cool floor. The dogs heard me and came rushing out of the living room. When I yanked open the front door, they crowded behind me, whining and nuzzling my legs. We walked out into the desert light.

I didn't hear Kit come up behind me. When he spoke, I jumped. How long had I been sitting on the porch steps? I scooted over, making room for him to pass, trying to pretend everything was fine.

"Hey, what are you doing out here?" he asked. "Where is everybody?" He sat down next to me, rubbing his face with his hands. His hair was sticking up in little coppery whirls.

"Just sitting," I said. I didn't want to answer the other

question. I couldn't think what to say. That they'd gone somewhere, Jamie and Beth? Her truck was still in the driveway.

"Where's Jamie?" he asked. He glanced around the yard. "Where's Beth?"

I hesitated. "Still sleeping, I guess." I looked at him. He was sitting so close to me, I could see the flecks of green and gold in his eyes. They were pretty, but in a complicated, surprising way, like the quartz inside a rock.

Kit frowned and glanced back into the house. I saw what he saw: the empty hallway and Beth's closed door. His eyes widened. He turned back to me.

"No way."

I pulled my knees up to my chin and swung my hair forward, hiding my face.

"No way!" he said again. This time, he grabbed my arm, making me look at him. "He's in there with her?"

I didn't say anything. I didn't have to. Kit whistled, and it was a low, wondering sound that pierced the air. "Unbelievable. Un-frigging-believable. I mean, we're stuck here in the middle of nowhere, thinking we might have *killed* that girl, and Jamie—" He shook his head. "Jamie gets laid."

"Stop," I said.

"No, I mean it." His mouth curved in a slow grin. "He has all the luck, you know?"

"It's not like that," I said. How did I know? Maybe it was like that.

93

"Oh, come on. He was totally into her. You saw it." Kit raked his hair back. "But I'm surprised she went for him. I thought she'd be all uptight about the age thing. What do you think happened? He crashed the same time I did."

I stared at my feet, curling my toes over the edge of the step. The wood was splintery.

Kit's hand clamped my shoulder. "Hey. You know something."

"No, I don't." I couldn't look at him.

"You totally do. You saw something. What?"

I tilted my chin down, shaking my head. "Nothing. I didn't see anything."

But Kit leaned toward me, pushing my hair back from my face. "Come on, Luce. Just tell me."

And then I wanted to tell him. It was too much to think about by myself. I looked up at him.

"Jamie was in the hallway," I said. "Late last night. He was ... upset. Upset about the girl, you know, and relieved, but—" I didn't want to say he was crying. Kit wouldn't understand that. "Beth came out of her room. I heard something, so I got up and started to open my door ... and I saw them."

"Yeah?" Kit said. "What'd she do?"

What had she done? How did it start? "She sort of hugged him—"

"She did?" Kit sounded incredulous. "She made the first move?"

94

No, that wasn't right. I shook my head. "She was trying to, you know, comfort him. And then he started kissing her."

Kit let out a long breath. "Wow. Really? And then what?"

"I don't know. I went back to bed."

"You're kidding! You missed the good part?"

I shoved him away. I knew I shouldn't have told him. "He's my *brother*! There is no good part. Beth is twice his age. It's ridiculous."

"Okay, okay. Relax." He shook his head. "It's still strange though, you know? Not Jamie, but Beth. She seems too – well, she must have known he liked her, so I'm surprised she'd do something—"

I couldn't take it. "Look, it's my fault. I told her you and Jamie were gay. That's why she hugged him. She didn't think it would start anything." There. I'd said it. I stared at the step.

"What?" Kit's voice was too loud.

"Shhh," I said. "They're still sleeping. You heard me. I told her you and Jamie were gay."

"Why the hell did you do that?" He was flushed and close to me. "What's the matter with you? Are you crazy? You think we're *gay*?" Suddenly he leaned forward and kissed me. Just like that. His mouth warm and mad on mine, but tight against it.

I couldn't believe it. I brought my hand up to his chest and pushed him away as soon as it started, but not soon enough. We sat there, inches from each other, breathing hard. I swallowed and wiped the back of my hand across my mouth. "I know you're not gay. And it's not like I'd care anyway. You don't have to … prove anything." That was all it was.

He turned away, but I was already sliding across the steps, shrinking back from him. I couldn't believe he'd kissed me. I could feel the hot sting of his mouth.

"Then why'd you say it? Why would you say something like that?" He wouldn't look at me.

I called for the dogs. They came trotting out of the shed, shaking their ears, looking sleepy and sweet. I made room for them between us. Oscar climbed the stairs and leaned heavily against my thigh. "I don't know. It didn't mean anything. I was mad at you guys for going to lunch without me. I never thought—"

"That's the problem. You don't think."

I frowned. That was interesting, coming from Kit.

"Look, it was a dumb thing to do. I'm sorry." I looped an arm around Oscar's neck and pressed my face into his fur. "Really. I wouldn't have said it if I thought anything like this might happen."

We both glanced back toward the hallway. The house was silent. Beth's door was still closed, and the air seemed to thicken around it, full of everything that had changed.

"You're crazy," Kit said.

He still wouldn't look at me. I couldn't believe he'd kissed me. Why had he done that? I knew he wasn't gay.

96

I'd seen him with girls for years, for almost as long as I'd known him. He always had a girlfriend.

I'd only been kissed once before. At the eighth-grade dance, the Friday before middle school graduation. Scott Lampere, who was kind of cute: tall and skinny, on the basketball team, with nice eyes. He was in three of my classes, and Ginny and I both liked him. But in a lazy way, never meaning to do anything about it. Plus, he had braces and some sort of wire mouthpiece that he had to wear for six months, so Ginny said kissing him would be like kissing the metal tab on a soda can.

But he got his braces off that spring. At the eighth-grade dance, he and I walked into the hallway to get something to drink, and he grabbed my arm and started kissing me. I was so surprised I didn't even know what to do. He had really wet lips, and they were sliding all over mine. I tried to cooperate, but the whole time he was kissing me, I was thinking about something I'd seen on TV. A show about the space program, about how, when a shuttle comes back to earth, if it doesn't enter the earth's atmosphere at exactly the right angle, it just bounces off into outer space. And that's what it felt like, kissing Scott: so slippery and uncertain that at any moment my mouth might slide off his and go flying into oblivion.

It was different when Kit kissed me. It felt smooth and snug, like the angle was exactly right.

16

"Let's go someplace," Kit said abruptly, standing up. "No point hanging around here. Let's get breakfast."

I nodded. I didn't really want to be in the house when Beth and Jamie finally opened the bedroom door. "But the car," I said. "Where did Jamie put the keys?"

"I don't know. We'll take her truck. The keys are on that hook in the kitchen. It's okay. She let us drive it yesterday. I mean, jeez, it's the least she can do, considering."

"Considering what? That she's in there with Jamie instead of you?" It surprised me how mean that sounded. "Forget it," I said quickly, before Kit could get mad again. "I guess she won't care."

We turned the corner into the kitchen and I stopped dead, Kit bumping into my back and almost knocking me down. Beth was standing at the sink, delicately peeling a tangerine. Her nails made neat scores in the rind, and she curled back the segments like petals. She glanced up when we came in. Her face was carefully blank, but everything else about her pulsed with feeling.

"Hi," she said.

I could barely look at her. Had she heard us talking? The bedroom door was closed. Jamie must still be sleeping. I could feel my face get hot. But why should I be embarrassed? She was the one who'd done something wrong.

"Hi," Kit said, stepping forward. "Can we borrow your truck? To get some breakfast?"

Now I glanced up. Her face seemed so controlled – I watched the calm arch of her eyebrows – as if the least sign of expression would reveal too much. "Sure," she said. "But you don't need to. There's plenty of food here."

"Well, we kind of feel like going out." Kit sounded casual. He smiled at her.

Beth turned away. She placed the half-peeled tangerine gently on the edge of the countertop, where it hovered like an exotic flower. "Okay," she said, wiping her hands on the dish towel. She took the keys from the hook on the wall and tossed them to Kit.

"Thanks."

I still hadn't said anything. I couldn't. Beth faced the window, gathering her hair with both hands and twisting it into a knot. A pink flush crept over her cheeks.

*   *   *

It wasn't until we were on the highway that Kit spoke, and his voice sounded glum. "They were probably screwing all night long."

"Stop it!" I reached across the seat to punch his shoulder. "Stop talking about it. It's too gross."

But there wasn't really anything else to talk about. I flattened my sketch pad on my lap and squinted out the window at the expanse of desert. The random thatches of grass seemed temporary, a futile defense against the dry ground. I wanted to draw them, but Kit was driving too fast and the highway was bumpy in spots.

"It was just a mistake, don't you think?" I said after a minute.

"I thought you didn't want to talk about it."

"I don't." I sighed, shifting in the seat, fiddling with the frayed strap of the seat belt. "But it won't happen again, right?"

Kit snorted. "Don't bet on it."

I winced. "How old do you think she is? She's got to be close to forty. Isn't that illegal or something?"

Kit's mouth twisted a little. "Everything fun is illegal."

"Come on, seriously." I was trying to think. There'd been something at the high school a few years ago. Some scandal. "Wasn't there a problem at Westview with a gym teacher a couple of years ago? And that girl, she was a junior or something. Didn't he get arrested?" Ginny and I were sixth-graders at the time, but I remembered my mom had been upset about it. I remembered her with Jamie in the kitchen, agitated, lowering her voice so I wouldn't hear.

"Well, yeah, Mr. Brimley. But that was totally different."

"Why? He was older. He was married."

"But it was a teacher-student thing. And the girl was fifteen, I think. Her parents sued."

"Well, how is this different?" I persisted. "Beth's too old for Jamie."

"It's just different." Kit shrugged. "Jamie wanted it."

"Maybe that girl wanted it, too. It's still wrong."

Kit shook his head. "It's different. With an older guy like that, the girl might not—" He stopped, glancing over at me. "I don't know. When the guy's older, like Mr. Brimley, and a teacher, it seems like the girl's more of a victim or something. Like it wasn't her choice." He paused. "Nobody forced Jamie, plus he's eighteen."

I settled back against the vinyl seat. That was true. I thought of Jamie's face in the moonlight, and the way he took Beth's hand.

"It's too weird," I said finally. "It should be illegal."

Kit grinned. "Don't be such a prude."

There was no point in talking about it with him. I looked out the window, watching the gravel shoulder blur by.

"Hey, which way are we going?" I asked suddenly.

He knew what I meant. "We passed it already," he said.

"We did? Was the police tape still there? I didn't see it."

"Yeah, it was still there."

"It feels like it's been more than two days, doesn't it? It seems so long ago."

He didn't say anything.

I flipped open my sketch pad and turned the pages till I came to the girl. I'd almost finished the drawing, but it wasn't quite right. The eyes and the mouth had no expression, and without that, her face just didn't look real. I kicked off my flip-flops and put my feet on the dashboard, angling the pad against my thighs. I started drawing again, hollows and ridges, the geography of cheekbones and brows. Faces were like landscapes.

"You draw all the time," Kit said. "What is that?"

I hesitated. "The girl."

He looked over now, quick glances, steadying the wheel with one hand. "Hey, that's pretty good," he said. That was the first nice thing he'd ever said to me.

"Thanks."

"The lips aren't right."

"What's wrong with them?" I mumbled.

He shrugged. "Something. Her mouth was different."

I looked at his mouth when he said that, and felt a rising flutter in my stomach. It was only Kit. But I kept thinking about how he'd kissed me. Part of me still couldn't believe it. Kit had *kissed* me. Kissed *me*. I snuck another glance at him, at the curve of his lips. I couldn't look at them without thinking how they felt against mine.

I went back to the drawing and erased the top of the girl's lip, changing the line to soften it. He was right. It looked more like her already.

"How far is this place?" I asked. "We've been driving forever." The desert was changing, turning to foothills with dark clumps of shrubs as we neared the mountains.

"I don't know. The restaurant Jamie and I went to yesterday was a lot closer. But it was in the other direction."

"Why'd you go this way then?" I turned to him impatiently. "I don't remember seeing anywhere to eat out here."

"Yeah." He looked sheepish. "I don't know. I wanted to drive by it again in the daylight."

"Oh." I nodded, wishing that I'd looked when we passed by. "What do you think happened to her?"

He was quiet, one hand gently shifting the steering wheel. "Somebody killed her."

Hearing him say it out loud made me shiver. I thought of the way I'd felt finding her body; the way I'd felt when I thought she'd died because of us. "But how? I mean, there wasn't any blood. Was there?" I didn't remember seeing anything like that. I stared at the face on the page, that lifeless oval. "I don't know. She seemed so calm."

"Yeah, but she was, what, in her twenties? People don't just die in their twenties."

"No, I guess not." He was right. She must have ended up there because of someone. Finding her was like finding half a picture ripped down the middle. What was on the other half?

Kit ran his fingers through his hair. It made red-gold waves across his head, cresting in curls at the nape of his neck. I gripped my pencil and went back to the sketch, shading the line of her throat.

Kit was still talking. "And you said the police didn't find anything on her, no wallet, no ID. That means somebody must have taken it."

I cringed, thinking of the bracelet. But there was no name on it, not even initials. It wouldn't have told them anything. Still, why had I done that? It was the same as stealing. I knew my mom would think that. So would Jamie.

"What if—" I stopped. The idea was forming in my head, and it seemed almost too fragile to say out loud, especially to Kit. "Listen, we're driving back in the same direction we came from that night. She was on the right side of the road. So whoever ... whoever left her there was probably driving the same way, you know? When we stop, we could ask if anyone saw her. We could try to find out—"

Kit was shaking his head. "No way. We're not doing that."

"Why? We have to stop anyway, for breakfast. There are so few places out here, maybe she went to one of them, too. You know, to get gas. Or eat. Why can't we just ask? Maybe someone saw her. I've got my sketch." I was talking faster now, pleading with him. "It's not the same as a photo, but you said yourself it's good, it looks like her. We could try to find out what happened to her."

Kit shook his head. "That's just dumb. What are you going to do, drive around the state showing people some drawing you did? Let the police figure it out. It doesn't have anything to do with us."

"But it does. We found her."

"And she was already dead! It's over. We'll be in Phoenix by tomorrow night."

"No! I'm not going to Phoenix. Not till we find out what happened to her." It sounded ridiculous even as the words came out of my mouth, but I realized I wasn't just saying it to argue with him. I meant it. I felt connected to her in some way, as though our lives had crossed and braided, even though she was a stranger. Or maybe because she was a stranger. Because she had come out of nowhere and might disappear into nowhere unless we tried to find out what had happened. "I'm not leaving her," I said quietly.

Kit looked at me in disgust. "You're crazy. And you know what? It's not up to you."

He turned the wheel sharply and we bumped off the highway into an unpaved parking lot. I hadn't been watching, but here it was, a little restaurant and mini-mart, a beige building with gas pumps in front and a rough wooden sign hanging from the roof: Blue Mountain Café. Kit swerved into a parking space, braking hard, and the pinkish-brown dust rose in clouds all around us.

17

Kit switched off the ignition.

"Kit," I said. "Can't we…" I gathered the pages of the sketch pad, flipping the cover closed and holding it against my chest.

"What?" He was frowning, impatient, but he was looking straight at me for the first time since he'd kissed me. I reached over and touched his arm. He flinched, his eyes flicking down to my hand. I realized with a start that he was nervous, too.

"Please," I said.

"Why does it matter to you? Why are you so obsessed with that girl?"

"I don't know." All I knew was that I couldn't stop thinking about her. "Don't you feel anything? I mean, she was left by the road, dead, and we were the ones to find her. Don't you feel … responsible for her somehow?"

"No! No, I don't." He jerked his arm away and got out of the truck. "Look, you do what you want. I'm not helping you." He slammed the door so hard the truck shook. I watched him stride across the parking lot to the restaurant, kicking up dust with each step. After a minute, I followed him.

I half expected he'd want to sit alone when we got inside, but when I walked in, I saw him watching me from a table in the corner, and he pushed out a chair with his foot.

"Thanks," I mumbled, looking around.

It was a small room with a dozen tables crowded close together and a long counter with stools at the back. The walls were dull pink, and the one behind Kit was covered with old calendars and photographs of different places, all of them lush and tropical. An older woman was frying hamburgers at the stove. Two men were sitting at the counter, but otherwise the place was empty.

The waitress came through a swinging door carrying two glasses of water. She had curly blond hair and crow's feet so deep her skin looked corrugated, like cardboard. Thick streaks of silver eye shadow glistened over her eyes. She slid the glasses across the table and took out a pad. "Hiya," she said. "What can I get for you kids?"

She smiled at Kit, and I watched him shake off his annoyance with me and smile back, a quick, warm grin. "You tell me," he said. "What's for breakfast?"

"Breakfast?" She laughed. "Not much. We stopped serving it at eleven."

"Oh," I said, "is it that late?" Nobody was listening to me.

Kit picked up the menu. "No pancakes?" He kept smiling at her.

"Well, I guess we could fix you some pancakes. But only because we're not busy." She glanced at me. "What can I get for your girlfriend?"

"I'm not his—"

"She's not my—"

We both said it so quickly, horrified, that she laughed again. "Okay, okay. My mistake. What can I get for you, hon?" She turned to me, pen poised.

"Scrambled eggs? With toast?"

"Sure. Juice?"

We both nodded. She started to turn away. "Wait," I said. I looked at Kit. "We were wondering—" He groaned and shook his head, but I flipped open the sketch pad and pushed it across the table before he could stop me. "Do you recognize this girl? She might have been here a couple of days ago."

The waitress looked at the page and then back at me, her face suddenly sharp. "That's a lot like the photo the police were passing around yesterday," she said. "Some poor girl that was killed on the highway. You kids know anything about it?"

"No," Kit said quickly. "Well, actually, we were the ones who found her, but we don't know anything. Lucy – this is my friend's sister" – he said this with a resigned roll of his eyes – "she had this idea that we could help the

108

police figure out what happened. But I told her they knew what they were doing. And since they've already talked to you" – he glared at me – "if we could just get some breakfast, that would be great."

The waitress seemed to relax again, clicking her pen and sliding it through the spiral ring of her pad. "Sure. Coming right up."

"Wait," I said again. "Sorry, but do you recognize her?" I didn't look at Kit. "Has she been here?"

The waitress shook her head. "No, hon. I've never seen her before."

"But—" I said. Kit kicked my shin under the table. "Ow!" I gave him a look. "But there aren't many restaurants around here, are there?"

The waitress slipped her pad in the pocket of her blouse. "No, nothing around here. Junie and I were talking with the police about that. There's a diner about an hour or so east, in Kilmore, toward the state line."

Kit frowned at me. "Anything else? Want to dust the place for fingerprints?"

The waitress winked at Kit. "I'll get those pancakes, hon."

"Jeez," Kit said when she left. "Will you give it up already? I told you the police would look into it. Stop hassling people."

"I wasn't hassling her. I was just asking. She didn't care."

I ran a finger across the water glass, making wavy lines in the condensation on the sides. I wanted to drive to Kilmore. But I knew better than to say anything about it to Kit.

18

We drove most of the way back to Beth's in silence. I had my pad open across my knees, and I sketched the mountains, just the silhouette of them, a jagged line rising over the horizontal sweep of land.

"How far away are they, do you think?" I asked Kit.

He shrugged. "An hour or two."

I hesitated, then said carefully, "Can we stop, when we come to the place where we found her?"

He looked over at me. "You can see it from the car."

"I know, but I want to get out."

"What *is* it with you?"

"Please?"

He sighed. "You are such a pain in the ass."

The land was so flat that we saw the yellow police tape from a long way off. It looked urgent in the distance, ribboning the side of the road. Kit slowed the truck and pulled onto the shoulder.

Everything seemed ordinary in the daylight. But even so, my chest tightened and my heart started to beat faster. The feeling was there, the same mounting dread from that night. I sat in the truck, unable to move.

"So? Don't you want to get out?" Kit asked impatiently.

I swallowed. "I don't know."

"Oh, come on, Luce!" He thumped his palm on the steering wheel. "You made me stop. Go take a look." When I still didn't move, he reached across my lap and unlatched the door. "Go on. Get it over with."

I climbed down from the cab and walked slowly toward the sagging tape. The word POLICE was printed all over it in sharp black letters. Even in the flat glare of the sun, the nothingness of the daytime, I was suddenly scared. It was stupid, I knew it. I kept moving my feet, one after the other, getting closer to the spot. In some deep part of me I believed that she'd still be lying there, dead, waiting to be found.

The yellow tape stretched over the low bushes to two plastic cones near the highway's edge. It blocked the shoulder. When I got to it, I stopped. I couldn't look. I felt the warm sun on my face and closed my eyes, trying to erase the panic from that night.

But then I heard the gravel crunch behind me, just as it had before, and I knew it was Kit. He stood next to me.

I could feel him looking at me. I opened my eyes and saw the white outline of her body on the ground. The crisp boundary of her life.

"Hey," Kit said. His voice was gentle, and so unlike him that I was afraid I might cry. "Luce."

"Don't be nice to me," I said desperately. "I can't take it."

"Okay." He turned me toward him, away from the bright yellow tape and the silhouette of her body. "Come on. Let's go."

His hand on my shoulder sent a warm ripple through me. And suddenly I wanted to block it all out. I thought of the night on the road, when I was sick to my stomach, how he'd held my hair. I wanted to think about something that wasn't the girl.

So I reached up and started kissing him.

It was different from the first time. Not hot and sudden that way. This time, his mouth was soft, startled. But almost immediately he started kissing me back. And when he kissed me I felt this fluttering, right through my center. I touched his hair, tangling my fingers in the curls at the back. His hands were on my shoulders, then on my face, holding it, tilting it toward him. I kissed and kissed him. I didn't want to stop. I could taste the sweet saltiness of his lips, feel his chest pressed against me. I couldn't think about anything else. When he finally pulled away, my mouth felt swollen, and it seemed as if my skin had been peeled back like a petal, leaving behind something raw and tingling and alive.

Kit stood there staring at me.

"We can't do this," I said. I couldn't look at him.

"Okay," he said.

"It's too—"

"Yeah," he said. "I know."

I started walking back to the truck.

"Luce."

"Let's just forget it, okay?" I tried to sound like I didn't care. "Now we're even."

I didn't even like Kit. And now I'd kissed him twice. Well, more than twice.

His mouth twitched. "Okay. Let's forget it."

"Fine."

"Great."

We swung open the doors to the truck simultaneously. There was no way I could forget it.

19

When we finally got back to Beth's, she was kneeling on the floor of the living room, painting, and Jamie was stretched across the couch watching her. Not just watching her. Riveted. Like he couldn't see anything else in the room. Kit and I made a lot of noise coming in. It wasn't deliberate exactly, but we both must have been thinking the same thing – that we didn't want to surprise them. We pushed the door open with a clatter, jangling keys and calling out, "Hey, we're back," in this loud, fake, sitcomish way. The dogs charged up to us, their nails scrabbling across the wooden floor. But Jamie never looked up.

"You were gone a long time," Beth said.

"Yeah. We went east," Kit said. "That place yesterday was a lot closer."

"The police called," she said after a minute.

"Oh yeah?" Kit glanced at me. "What did they want?"

"They've got the coroner's preliminary report. They know the cause of death." Beth sat back on her heels, looking at both of us, and Jamie suddenly stood, catapulting off the couch.

"Yeah, listen to this," he said.

"What?" I asked.

"She just died."

"Huh?" Kit said. "What do you mean?"

"Congenital heart disease," Beth said. "She had a heart attack. Incredibly rare for someone her age, but it happens. She died instantly, the police said."

"You mean she wasn't killed?" Kit asked. "Nobody did anything to her?"

I turned to him. "Somebody left her there."

Beth nodded. "Yes. Somebody did that, and the police still don't know who. They haven't been able to find out anything about her." She hesitated. "But the death itself, it looks like natural causes. So—" She lifted her paintbrush and held it absently in midair, looking at Jamie. "You can go anytime you want."

"We can?" Kit said eagerly. "That's great!" He checked his watch. "If we leave now, we can get to Phoenix by midnight."

We could go. It seemed impossible. We could just drive away, leaving all this behind. I thought of the bracelet, hidden in the pocket of my backpack. I thought of Jamie and Beth together last night, and of Kit kissing me.

115

Part of me wanted so badly to leave. It had only been two days. We could get back on the road, have everything return to normal. It would be a relief, pure and simple, to sit in the hot back seat and listen to Kit and Jamie talk.

But part of me didn't. I felt a pit open in my stomach. It wasn't finished. Nobody knew who she was, nobody knew what had happened to her. We were the ones who'd found her. We couldn't just leave.

"We can't just leave," said Jamie.

"What?" Kit looked at him. "Sure we can."

"No," I said. "I don't want to."

Now Jamie looked at me, not understanding, but grateful. Beth didn't say anything. She was watching him, her paintbrush dripping noiselessly onto the cloth.

"You two are out of your minds," Kit said. "What about your dad? What about our spring break?"

"I'm not going," Jamie said.

"Jamie—" Kit shook his head, looking from Jamie to Beth. "What the—?" He turned to me.

"Me neither," I said quietly.

Kit started to say something, then changed his mind. He sank heavily into the couch, exhaling loudly.

"This is nuts," he said, looking at the three of us. "I hope you know what you're doing."

Nobody answered him. There was nothing to say.

Later that afternoon, I lay across the bed in the blue bedroom, pressing the phone close to my mouth and talking to Ginny. There was too much to tell her, and this time saying it aloud made it seem more absurd, like I was making it up. I started with the girl.

"Wow," Ginny said. "But that's *great*. I mean, I thought Jamie was going to jail, for sure. I thought we'd be visiting him in, like, a New Mexico *prison*. Can you imagine? And now it's just nothing."

"It's not nothing," I said. "She's still dead."

"I know, I know," Ginny said hurriedly. "And it's so bizarre. Whoever heard of dying when you're twenty? That is freaky. I didn't mean it's nothing-nothing. I just mean you can go to your dad's now. You know?"

"We can't," I said. "Not yet."

"Why not?"

I considered all the possible answers to that question, and finally blurted out, "Jamie slept with Beth."

I could hear her rustling with interest. "What?"

"Jamie. He slept with Beth."

"Who's that?"

"The lady who lives here, at the house where we're staying. I told you about her. The artist."

"But I thought you said—"

"Yeah, she's old. As old as…" I didn't want to say my mom.

Ginny blew out a long, impressed breath. "Wow. He *slept* with her? Are you sure? Maybe they just made out."

I sighed. "No, I don't think so." I told her what had happened in the hallway.

"Wow," she said again.

"And Kit kissed me." I added this quickly, going for broke. I might as well tell her everything.

"What?" She shrieked into the phone, and I could hear the springs of her mattress squeak as she bounced on the bed.

"I know."

"Kit the *zit*? You're kidding."

"No, I'm not. And you can't call him that anymore."

"Lucy! No way!"

I sighed. "It's true."

"Holy shit. What is going on down there? I think you guys need to come back to Kansas *pronto*."

"We do," I said fervently. "We really do. But we can't yet."

"Wait, stop. Tell me about kissing *Kit*. What was it like? How did that even *happen*?"

"I don't know. It was just—" I felt shy about it suddenly. "It was nice," I said finally.

"Better than Scott Lampere?"

"Well, of course. Duh."

"Okay, okay. But still. I just can't see it. Kit's always so mean. He can be *horrible*. And he never even looks at us. I thought he couldn't stand us."

"Me too," I said.

Ginny waited a minute. When I didn't say anything, she sighed. "Well, I guess he changed his mind. Which is good." I could hear her reevaluating. Kit was being reborn in her mind. "I mean, he is cute. You have to admit."

"Uh-huh."

"He's really cute, actually."

"I know."

"With that hair. His girlfriends are always pretty."

"Yeah."

"So do you think you and Kit—?"

"No. No, it's not like that. It was just one kiss." I could feel myself blushing with the lie, but I couldn't tell her about the second time. That seemed like something else entirely.

"But I still don't get how it started. With you and Kit."

"It was dumb," I said. I explained how I'd told Beth that Jamie and Kit were gay. "So I think he did it just to prove something."

"Oh." Ginny sounded disappointed. "So you don't think he'll kiss you again?"

"No," I said firmly. "That was it."

"Well…" She paused, delicately. "Do you *want* him to kiss you again?"

"I don't know," I said. I could hear her waiting on the other end, breathing into the phone. I hesitated. "I might."

She squealed again, dissolving in a fit of giggles. "You *kissed* Kit! *Kit!* I can't believe it. This is so great." She sighed. "I wish I were there."

"I do, too," I said. I really did.

20

All afternoon, I watched Jamie and Beth. Or watched Jamie watching Beth. There was nothing obvious between them – they didn't kiss or hug, or even touch each other – but at the same time, there was no mistaking what had happened. Jamie had a look on his face that I'd never seen before. His eyes followed Beth's every movement, like she was something he wanted to study and learn by heart. And Beth seemed as changed as he did. The force of his gaze seemed to be polishing her, right in front of us, making her smooth and graceful, making her skin shine. She looked beautiful.

Kit saw it, too. When I went into the kitchen to get a drink, he followed me, looking morose. "God, she really is hot," he said. "Who cares how old she is?"

I shuddered. "You have to talk to him."

"And say what? Congratulations? You scored?"

"No! You have to stop it."

He snorted. "Uh-uh. That's your department. You're the prude."

"Stop saying that." He was looking at me, smiling a little, and I could feel my cheeks getting hot. "I'm not a prude," I said, frustrated.

"Okay, maybe not," he said. "But about this, you are."

"Come on, he's my brother! I don't want him to get in trouble."

Kit smirked. "It doesn't look like trouble to me. But if you're so worried about it, you talk to him."

I sighed, steeling myself. "Tell him to come in here. We need to call our dad." That was true. He was expecting us in Phoenix tomorrow. But I knew Jamie wouldn't want to talk to him any more than I did. Neither of us could tell him the real reason we were staying.

Jamie came through the doorway looking flushed and impatient. "What's up?"

I tried to see him, just for a minute, the way Beth must see him, with his dark hair falling over his forehead and the bright warmth in his eyes. Jamie's eyes were always full of whatever he was feeling, in a way other people's weren't.

But it was too hard to see him as a stranger. Everything about him was familiar. It was hard to even see him as cute. I knew the girls at school thought so, but it wasn't something I ever considered. It was impossible to imagine him as a person you'd fall in love with.

"We have to call Dad," I said. "He still thinks we're on our way to Phoenix, remember? He's going to be mad."

Jamie rubbed his face, frowning a little. "I talked to him last time."

"Yeah, but I was the one who made the phone call."

"You just left a message."

"Still. It's your turn."

Jamie sighed. "He always asks me a ton of questions. If you call, he won't bug you as much about why we're not leaving."

That was probably true, but I didn't want to do it.

"You call him. You're the oldest."

Jamie bit his lip, looking out the window. "I'll try the office," he decided. "He's probably not even there."

So finally he called, pacing back and forth across the kitchen while our dad's office phone rang loudly enough for me to hear it on the other side of the room. I could tell from the quickness in Jamie's voice that he had gotten the answering machine. "Hey, Dad. We're still here in New Mexico, and ... and it looks like we're going to be here awhile longer. There's no problem with the police or anything, and the car's fine. But it's just ... it's taking longer than we thought. So we'll call you again when we know more. Sorry. Hope this doesn't, um, mess up your plans. Bye." Jamie banged the phone down.

"Did you give him the phone number here?"

"No." Jamie looked at me. "Do you really want him to call back?"

"No, I guess not."

He started to go back to the living room, but I caught his arm. "Jamie."

"What?"

"This thing with Beth—"

"What about it?"

"You have to stop."

His face closed down, immediately.

"She's too old for you."

He looked at me impassively.

"It was just, like, a mistake." I tried again. "I know you didn't mean for it to happen. But you can't keep it up."

"I did mean for it to happen," Jamie said. "And it's none of your business."

"But, Jamie," I protested. "Jeez. Think about it. I mean, Mom and Dad would go ballistic over this."

"It's none of their business either," he said. "It's nobody's business."

"But it's—"

"Luce," he said, his voice quiet, but as final as a door slamming shut. "I'm not going to talk about it. Okay?" He left the kitchen, and I stood next to the table, digging my fingernails into the white wood.

21

"It didn't work," I said to Kit later that evening, as we were cleaning up the dishes. We'd volunteered because Beth had cooked for us – barbecued chicken, corn on the cob – and she and Jamie had husked the corn and mixed the sauce and done the grilling, while Kit and I hung back, not sure how to fit into their easy collaboration. It was like they'd been together for years. I kept expecting to see something in Jamie, some sign that he felt embarrassed or awkward or ashamed. But he didn't even seem to notice we were there.

Once, when I was setting the table in the kitchen, I glanced out the window and saw him grab Beth's waist and kiss the back of her neck – so comfortably that it stopped me short. She closed her eyes and leaned her head back, sliding her palm over his face.

After dinner, as we were stacking the dirty plates next to the sink, Jamie said, "Let's take a walk." At first I'd thought he meant all of us, but when I turned and started to answer, he was looking only at Beth.

So now it was seven o'clock and Kit and I were standing in the kitchen with a sink full of gray, sudsy water, watching Jamie and Beth cross the yard in the blue dusk, their blurred shapes moving closer together as they got farther from the house.

"What didn't work?" Kit asked.

"Talking to Jamie. He won't listen to me."

"You must be used to that."

"Yeah." I wiped my hands on the dish towel. "But this is important. He knows I'm right."

"How do *you* know you're right?"

I glared at him. "About this? I just am."

"Because you're always right."

"I didn't say that."

"That's what you're thinking."

"No, I wasn't. I wasn't thinking that at all." I dumped the corncobs in the wastebasket and banged the lid closed. "Quit picking on me." I handed him the scraped plates.

The line of his jaw tightened. He didn't seem like he was joking. "Just like you were right in the car that night, when we hit something. You said we had to turn around and find out what it was. Look how well that worked out."

I swallowed. "What do you mean?" He loaded the last two plates into the dishwasher, his forearms wet and gleaming.

He looked at me. "That girl had nothing to do with us. And if we'd kept driving, if we'd driven to Albuquerque, we wouldn't have gotten in trouble with the police. We'd never have met Beth. Jamie wouldn't have slept with her. We'd have been in Phoenix the next day and right now, instead of being stuck here, we'd be spending spring break with your dad." He slammed the dishwasher shut and took the towel from me, roughly wiping his hands. "Which would be a hell of a lot more fun than this."

I stared at him. "So now you're blaming everything on me?"

"Well?"

"It's not my fault the girl was dead."

"No. But it's your fault we found her."

I turned before he could see my face and ran back to the bedroom, kicking the door shut behind me.

I lay on my stomach with my face against the pillow, breathing the clean smell of the sheets, trying not to cry. I didn't know why I was surprised. Of course that was what Kit thought. I'd ruined his spring break. I'd ruined everyone's spring break, and more than that. Jamie was in this mess because of me.

Kit and I had kissed and kissed – it made me tremble just to think about it – but it didn't change who he was.

126

He was still Kit. And I was still me.

I wanted to talk to my mom. Not to tell her anything, I couldn't do that. But just to hear her voice. She was working tonight, the evening shift at the clinic. I took the phone and punched her number.

"Women's Healthcare Associates."

I sighed, leaning into the calm of her voice. "Mom, it's me."

"Oh! Honey, how are you? *Where* are you? Are you headed for your father's?"

"No, not yet."

"But why not? Aren't things cleared up there? Your father talked to the sheriff this afternoon. He said you were free to go."

"Yeah, we are…" I hesitated.

"What's wrong? What's happened?"

"Nothing, Mom. Nothing happened. It's just—"

The other line beeped. "Oh, hold on a second, Lucy." I waited.

"What were you saying, honey? Why haven't you left for Arizona?"

"It's just that the police don't know anything about the girl yet. They didn't find an ID or anything. And it looks like she died of a heart attack."

"Yes, I know. Your father told me. It's so strange. Terrible. Poor thing, and her family – they must not even know she's dead yet. I can't imagine it." I could feel her shuddering. "Oh, hold for a second."

I waited, listening to the steady beeps.

"Lucy?"

"You're busy. I can call you later."

"I won't be home till midnight, honey. It'll be too late. But I still don't understand why you haven't left. Is everything okay?" The phone beeped again, but this time she ignored it, waiting for me to answer.

I hesitated. Nothing was okay. "Yeah, Mom. By the time we heard from the police, it was so late, you know?" I took a deep breath. "We didn't want to drive at night."

"Oh. Well, that makes sense, especially after what happened. So you'll leave first thing tomorrow? How's Jamie? Does he seem better?"

I swallowed. "I think he's still kind of shook up."

"Well, put him on for a minute. And then I should go. The phones are ringing off the hook here."

"He—" I hesitated. "He's outside. He went for a walk."

"He did?" I could hear the flicker of doubt in her voice. "Are you sure everything's okay, Lucy?"

"Yeah, we're fine. I just wanted to talk to you, that's all. I'm sorry I called you at work."

"No, no, I'm glad you did. Call me tomorrow, okay? Love you, honey."

I set the phone down and listened to the silence in the room. I wondered what my mom would say if I told her everything. What she'd *do*. That was the thing about telling your parents anything important. They never just listened, they always had to do something about it. Which

128

sometimes only made things worse.

I reached down and tugged my backpack across the floor to the bed, unzipping the inside pocket. Carefully, I drew out the bracelet. The silver gleamed. The little charms danced and clinked against each other. With one finger, I tapped the horseshoe, watching it turn. I dropped the bracelet on the blanket beside me. I thought of the girl's slim wrist, and how easy it had been to unfasten the bracelet and slide it into my pocket.

Maybe everything was my fault. But how could you ever know the right thing to do? If you could somehow see what was going to happen, it would be different. Then you wouldn't make these mistakes. I'd never have told Beth that Jamie was gay, because I'd have known exactly where it might lead. But at the time, it had seemed such a small thing, so unconnected to anything else. Like taking the bracelet. Like looking through the rain-splashed window of the car that night and saying, "We have to go back."

I touched the delicate surface of each charm. There weren't so many choices, were there? Once we found her, we had to do something. We couldn't leave her there, alone like that, on a highway in the rain. She was somebody's daughter. Maybe somebody's sister. Just because she was dead didn't mean she didn't matter.

I heard Kit's footsteps in the hallway and closed my fist over the bracelet, shoving it under my stomach on the bed.

"Luce?" He sounded impatient, not sorry.

I didn't say anything.

"What are you doing in there?"

I burrowed my face into the pillow and mumbled, "Nothing. Go away."

The door swung open. "I can't hear you," he said, walking over to the bed. When I opened one eye and squinted up at him, I thought he did look a little sorry. But I turned my face away, clutching the bracelet tight beneath me. He sat down on the bed, the springs creaking, and my heart began to beat a little faster.

"What are you mad about?" He put his hand on my back, fanning it over my ribs. I could feel my skin leaping up to meet his fingers, tingling under their warmth. I shivered.

"You're jumpy." It was the voice he used with the waitress. "What, am I making you nervous?"

"No," I said, still not looking at him. "You don't make me nervous."

"You sure?" He swept my hair away from my face and leaned close to me, his breath on my cheek. His hand moved in slow circles over my back. I stiffened.

"I thought we weren't going to do this," I said.

"Do what?" His voice was soft. He started kissing me, rolling me toward him, his mouth on my face and my lips, and suddenly I was pressed against him and reaching up with both hands to hold him, to hold myself and keep the room from spinning.

I remembered too late about the bracelet. It dropped

from my hand and clattered on the floor.

I pulled back, catching my breath.

And that was my mistake. If I'd kept kissing him, Kit would never have noticed. But now he lifted his head and glanced over the edge of the bed. "What was that?" he said.

I bit my lip. He wouldn't recognize it.

He picked it up and brought it onto the bed, laying it between us on the cover. His brows came together. "Is it yours?" he asked uncertainly.

I could have lied, gathering the words to make him believe me. He would never have known.

But I wanted him to know. That was the thing about lying. In the end, it was so lonely.

I shook my head slowly.

He kept looking at the bracelet. With his index finger he shaped it into a circle. "Beth's?" he asked. Then, frowning, "No. Wait." He raised his eyes, and they were full of wonder. "It's hers."

I nodded.

"You took her bracelet?"

I nodded again.

"That's messed up."

I pressed my face against his shoulder. "I know," I said into his shirt.

22

The urge to stay like that, with my cheek against his shirt, was so powerful that I couldn't bring myself to move. But I didn't have a choice. Kit pushed me back, tilting my face up so he could look at me.

"You stole her bracelet? Off her *body*?"

It sounded so much worse when he said it that way. I couldn't answer him.

"But why? Why'd you do that?"

I rolled backward on the bed and covered my face with my hands. "I don't know! I don't know."

He didn't say anything. When I spread my fingers to see what he was doing, he was staring at the bracelet, lifting each charm and turning it in his hand.

"I didn't mean to," I said hopelessly.

Kit just looked at me.

"Okay, I meant to, but not to steal it. I—" I stopped. He wouldn't understand. No one would understand. "I wanted to keep it safe. You know? The police were coming and I knew they would take her away and I just wanted to—" How could I explain it? I didn't even understand it myself.

"When did you take it? I didn't see you."

"No. You and Jamie were talking to Beth. It was right before the ambulance came."

"This is so messed up," he said again. "The police said she didn't have any ID on her. Something like this could be important."

"I know. I know." I touched his hand, and his fingers immediately curved over mine, so the bracelet was pressed between our palms. The warmth of his skin sent little prickles through me. "But if I tell them now, if I try to give it back ... isn't it stealing? Won't I get in trouble?"

He turned my hand over and uncurled my fingers, lifting the bracelet. It swung in the air between us, inches from my face. The room was almost dark now. I could barely see it, or Kit's expression. I couldn't tell what he was thinking.

I swallowed. "Should I tell them?"

He shook his head. "I don't know."

I lay back on the bed again, turning away from him. "What if it's some kind of clue? Would it help the police figure out who she was?"

The mattress shifted and I felt him sink down beside me, his shoulder almost touching mine, but not quite, so there was a charged silhouette of space all around me, thin and electric. After a while, his voice came out of the darkness. "Is there anything on it? I mean, besides the charms?"

"No. No name, nothing like that. I checked. Just charms. The kind you get at jewelry stores. At the mall." I pointed to the silver heart. "I have one just like that on my charm bracelet at home."

"Then maybe it wouldn't matter anyway." I knew he was trying to make me feel better.

I looked out the window at the blue-black night. "It's the worst thing I've ever done," I said hollowly.

Kit snorted, sounding like himself again. "No way."

"It is. I stole something from a *dead* person."

"Oh, come on. You must have done worse things than that."

"No. Really." I turned slightly, watching his fuzzy profile in the dark, feeling the warmth of his body close to mine. "What's the worst thing you ever did?"

He started to laugh, but suddenly I wanted to know. It seemed important. "Tell me," I said.

"Are you serious? That would take all night."

"Not everything," I said, frustrated. "Just the worst thing. Please." I was almost whispering. "I told you mine."

Kit turned toward me and his face was inches away on the pillow. I watched his lips move in the dark, softly changing shape. "The worst thing? Jeez."

"And not one of those stunts you and Jamie pulled at school, either."

134

He was quiet for a minute. Then he clasped his hands behind his head and stared at the ceiling. "Okay. The worst thing…" In the last bit of light coming through the window, I could see him chewing on his lower lip. "Last year, Jamie and I were out at a bar, late—"

Immediately, I wished I hadn't asked him. Of course it would involve Jamie, and it wouldn't be something I wanted to hear. "You mean drinking?"

"Uh, yeah, that's generally what you do at a bar. But not around home, you know? Not where someone would recognize us. We were over in Winston." Winston was almost an hour away, a small town with a community college, mostly farm kids, and a tiny, run-down main street. "And we'd been there awhile – two, three hours – when this guy comes in with a really pretty woman, a redhead. They're a little drunk, kissing, and everybody's looking at them, and…" He stopped.

"What?"

"And it was my dad."

I stared at him. Kit's parents were both good-looking in a glossy, sophisticated way, like an ad for a country club.

"But…"

"Yeah. My dad. With this woman. He didn't see us, you know, so we snuck out. Right away. I mean, Jamie and I didn't want to get caught."

"Oh," I said. "No."

"But then, afterwards, I knew this thing about my dad. And I was mad, right? I mean, it wasn't like a huge shock.

135

I kind of figured he was sleeping around. But what was he thinking, going to Winston, which is only an hour away, with some other woman? Anybody could have seen him. What's up with that?" He straightened one arm over his head and tapped his knuckles against the wall.

"So I thought I should tell my mom." His mouth curved down sharply. "He was making a fool of her, you know? I mean, why should she sit around ironing his shirts and fixing his dinners when all the time he's just…"

I leaned toward him, watching his face. I wanted to fix the angry twist of his mouth, to smooth it away. "You don't have to tell me," I said.

"No, listen. So I'm nervous about it, right? Like, who wants to tell their mom *that*? But one day I just say it. I tell her the whole thing, how we were in the bar, what we saw."

He hesitated.

"What happened?" I whispered.

"She slapped me. Right across the face. She said, 'Who the hell do you think you are, telling me something like that?' "

I stared at him.

"And that was it. We never talked about it again."

Suddenly it seemed like nothing to reach across the charged gap between us and slip my hand into his, holding it tight. I'd known him for years, but maybe I hadn't known him at all. You could spend months and months with a person and not learn anything about them, compared with what you found out in a few minutes, with one story. Maybe everyone had one story that explained who they really were.

"Kit," I said, curling close to him, leaning my forehead against his shoulder. "That's not the worst thing you ever did. That's the worst thing they ever did."

"No," he said, his voice hard. "I shouldn't have told her. It wasn't any of my business. And it could have wrecked things between them. Maybe it did."

"Why was she so mad at you? Did she think it wasn't true?"

He shook his head. "That's what I thought at first, that she didn't believe me. But then I thought, no, she believes me. She already knows. And I wasn't supposed to let on that I knew, because then it was just too hard ... to keep the whole thing going. She thought it was, I don't know, disrespectful, or something. For me to tell her about my dad."

I squeezed his hand in the dark. "I'm sorry," I said.

"Yeah. Well, shit happens."

In the yard we heard the loud burst of the dogs barking, and then voices coming closer. "They're back," I whispered, sitting up. "You'd better get out of here."

He looked at me silently for a minute, then got to his feet in one motion and left the room.

23

I slipped out of my clothes in the dark and dropped the bracelet into my backpack. I could hear Jamie and Beth in the hallway. I couldn't hear what they were saying, just the low, flowing river of their words, blending and separating, punctuated by her soft laughter, the rush of his response.

He's falling in love with her, I thought.

How could that be? It was too soon. But I could feel it.

I crawled under the cool sheets, straining to follow their voices in the stillness. After a while, I heard them open the door to Beth's room and go inside. When the door closed, the sound was firm and final, like a lid snapping shut. It sealed Jamie in, separating him from Kit and me.

I had another dream about the girl. I saw the road and

heard the heavy rain, just as I had the past two nights. I was starting to think I'd never really sleep again. Sometimes I couldn't even tell if I'd slept until the dream came, so real that I woke up shaking.

This time the girl rose, glowing in the headlights, with her arms outstretched and her lips moving. I tried so hard to hear what she was saying, but her voice was muffled. I knew she was asking for some kind of help. But before I could figure out what she wanted, the car slammed into her.

I bolted upright, breathing hard. My watch said 2:00 a.m.

I lay back down, holding the sheets close to my chin, listening to the quiet house. I could hear faint rustlings in the kitchen. Maybe it's Jamie, I thought. Maybe I could try to talk to him again.

But when I got to the kitchen doorway, the person I saw was Beth.

She looked otherworldly in the dark, her nightgown sliding over a bare brown shoulder. It didn't seem like the kind of nightgown she'd wear. It was so delicate, and there was nothing delicate about Beth, with her paint-splotched hands and quick competence. She was standing at the sink, staring out the window.

I held the doorjamb to steady myself and said, "You have to stop."

"Oh!" She turned, hugging her arms against her stomach. "Lucy, I didn't hear you. What are you doing up?"

"I had a bad dream."

"What about?"

I shrugged. "Please," I said. "You have to stop. Jamie's too young."

She looked at me, a long guarded look. "I know that."

"Please," I tried again. "I know he's – I know he's cute, and you probably never meet anybody out here, but—"

"It's not what you think."

I swallowed. "I know what it is. I can see, okay? I can see how he feels about you. And—" I stopped, then said the rest in a rush. "And you're too old!"

She drew back, her brows contracting.

But I couldn't stop now. If I couldn't make Jamie understand, at least I could convince Beth. "You have to stop it. I mean, you're the grown-up. He just turned eighteen. You know that, right? He's going to graduate in two months. He's going to the University of Illinois next fall. He has a whole life back home … girlfriends and sports and a job."

She didn't say anything. She wasn't looking at me anymore.

I gripped the wood of the door frame. "I mean, what about being responsible? What about thinking of the consequences?" I sounded like the Health Ed teacher at school, with her grim moralizing about safe sex.

"Consequences," said Beth. She shook her head. "I know how it seems to you. But Lucy, the thing is—" She stopped. "You know something? Everybody says you get more cautious as you get older, more afraid of change. But it isn't true. The truth is, you get bolder. You don't think about whether it's dangerous, because you might not get another chance." She closed her eyes and pressed her fingers against her forehead, kneading the skin. "There are consequences to everything. Not just the things you do, but the things you don't do."

I stared at her.

"But why Jamie? Why not somebody else? Somebody who lives here, the sheriff, somebody your own age." It sounded desperate even to me.

She kept looking out the window. "I didn't plan it," she said. "I thought he was gay, remember?" She glanced at me, but there was nothing accusing in her eyes, just a kind of quiet understanding. "You know something? I was never lonely here," she continued. "Not ever. Until Jamie. Then, I don't know why, I was so lonely I couldn't stand it."

I could feel the sense of panic tightening around my chest like a fist. "But that's what it is for you," I said. "Not for Jamie. He's not lonely. He's just a kid." I watched the back of her head dip slightly. I hesitated. "I think he's falling in love with you."

Beth didn't look at me. Her voice was subdued. "I know."

I couldn't stand it. "You're taking advantage of him. It isn't fair. You're going to hurt him."

She flinched, as if I'd hit her, and finally turned to face me, her cheeks flushed. "I can't talk to you about this," she said. She walked past me down the hall to her room.

I stood trembling in the kitchen. It came to me suddenly, with the slap of truth, that I couldn't stay here anymore. I couldn't stay in this house and watch whatever was going to happen between them. It was too hard. And the only way to leave was to get Kit to take me.

The hallway was shrouded in darkness. I felt for the door to the study and paused outside it, feeling my heart kick in my chest. Then I pushed it open.

Kit lay on his back, his chest bare, a half-folded blanket dragged indifferently across him. His breathing was steady. The moon was a bright, unblinking eye outside the window, casting soft light on his face.

"Kit," I whispered.

He didn't move.

I knelt beside him and hesitantly put my hand on his shoulder. The skin was warm, dense with muscle.

"Kit," I said again, louder.

There was no response. His breathing didn't change at all.

I thought of the girl, and I felt cold and afraid. I lay down on the floor, close to him. "Kit, what's going to happen to us?" I whispered, my mouth against his shoulder.

He still didn't move. I kept watching his profile for any sign that he heard me. I breathed his thick, sweet smell, the smell of his hair and his neck and his sleeping self, all mixed together. I put my hand on his chest to feel the thudding of his heart.

And then he stirred, shifted slightly, turning toward me. One hand reached sleepily for me, running over my body, feeling me through my T-shirt. I curled against him. He was touching me, his hands warm, and I thought

142

– in the way your body knows things that your mind will only guess – *he's done this lots of times*.

"Kit," I said again.

"What?" His voice was soft. "What are you doing in here?"

"I want to leave." I touched his face. "I want to go to Kilmore."

His eyes were still closed but his hand slid down my arm in one stroke, encircling my wrist. "What are you talking about?" he mumbled.

"I can't stay here anymore. Please, Kit. Can we go? Can we go to Kilmore?" I moved my lips against his skin and I felt dizzy, unable to think, but I had to hear him say yes.

"Okay, okay. But don't talk about it now," he whispered, pulling me closer. "In the morning."

I wove my fingers through his hair. "No, now. I want to leave now."

His eyes opened then. He drew back from me, his hand still holding my wrist. "What?"

"We have to leave now," I said.

He frowned. "Why?"

I got to my knees, yanking my T-shirt down, shivering. "I can't stay here anymore. If you won't take me, I'll drive myself." I looked straight at him to make sure he'd believe me.

He sat up slowly, wiping his hand over his face. "What are you talking about? You don't know how to drive."

I tried not to stare at his chest. "I do! Enough. I know

enough to drive to Kilmore." It wasn't true. I'd only been out a few times with my mom, in parking lots and dead-end streets. I wouldn't have my license for another year.

He shook his head, looking at me more closely now. I couldn't meet his gaze. "But what's going on? I mean, jeez, why the fire drill?"

I couldn't answer. So I did the thing that later I wished I hadn't. I leaned toward him and looped my arm around his neck and pulled his face toward mine. I kissed him, and I kept kissing him until I felt his hesitation melt away in the darkness and I couldn't tell where my face ended and his began. And this time, what happened between us wasn't an accident or a surprise. It was a choice.

When we finally stopped, all he said was "Okay."

I don't know if it was the kissing that did it, or if he understood somehow, or if he knew he wasn't going to change my mind. But whatever the reason, he pushed back the blanket and started gathering his things together, stuffing them into his duffel bag. And I could hardly believe it: there we were, stumbling around in the dark, tiptoeing past the room where Beth and Jamie slept, and leaving a quick scribbled note for Jamie on the kitchen table.

I threw chicken scraps in the dogs' bowls to keep them from barking when we left. Kit found Jamie's keys in the study and slipped his cell phone into the pocket of his jeans. We crossed the yard in the predawn stillness, climbing into the cold car for the first time since the accident.

We were going to Kilmore.

24

It was a long drive on the dark road that stretched to the horizon. Almost immediately we came to the place where we'd found the girl, but we roared past.

I was sitting next to Kit. Not all the way over on the passenger side, but next to him, because it had seemed the most natural thing when we got into the car. He drove with one hand on the wheel, the other one resting on my leg, just above my knee. His thumb made lazy circles on my thigh.

He glanced over at me. "So what's the big plan, when we get to Kilmore?"

I could tell he was teasing me, but I didn't care. "We'll go to the restaurants, the stores, whatever's there. And we'll show them the sketch and ask, you know, if anybody saw her. We'll just see what we can find out."

His thumb kept stroking my leg. "So tell me why that will work. Why do you think we'll find out something the police don't already know?"

"Because … well, maybe we'll think of something they haven't." I sighed. "It's better than hanging around Beth's watching Jamie ruin his life, isn't it?"

"Who says he's ruining his life?"

I didn't want to fight about it. I laced my fingers through his, lifting his hand into my lap. "I know you think I'm—" I stopped. "Overreacting. But he's my brother, okay? And come on. You can't think it's normal to sleep with somebody who's twenty years older than you are. Are you telling me it doesn't freak you out at all? Not even a little?"

Kit shrugged. "Not really. I mean, believe me, it would if she were ugly. But she's not. I can kind of see it. She's really sure of herself. She knows what she's doing."

I waited, but he didn't say anything else. "That's it? That's enough to make Jamie sleep with her?"

"Well, yeah. It's the whole package. She puts herself out there, you know? Says what she thinks. Looks you in the eye." He laughed at my expression. "What? It's not only about boobs. Jeez."

"But that's all you and Jamie talk about," I protested.

"Yeah, of course. But there's more to it than that."

I sighed. "Okay, maybe that explains Jamie. But what about her? What does she see in him?"

Kit snorted. "He's eighteen. She's over-the-hill. I think it's pretty obvious."

146

I shook my head. "No, she doesn't seem like that." I thought about the way Jamie looked at her, and how that must make her feel. I wondered if you could fall in love with someone's image of you; some version of yourself, reflected back.

"Don't worry about it," Kit said. "It's not like he's going to move to New Mexico and have a bunch of kids with her. He's just, you know, having a good time. You can't blame him for that. Or her."

I didn't say anything. There was no point.

Around us the darkness was changing, turning blue, then gray, then a violet-pink on the horizon. The desert was streaked with color. The shadowy mountains gathered closer.

I leaned over the back seat and found my sketch pad, then scooted closer to the window to draw.

"Hey, where are you going?" Kit reached down to grab my ankle.

I laughed at him, letting his fingers curl around my foot. "I was going to draw the mountains. But maybe I'll draw you instead."

"What, from the side?"

"Yeah, a profile. It's easier, actually." I leaned against the car door with my feet resting on his leg, sketching quickly, the pencil making soft scratching sounds on the page. Part of me couldn't believe this was really Kit Kitson. I studied his smile, his messy hair. I liked the loose constellation of freckles that covered his cheeks; they made

147

him seem younger. The pencil moved without stopping, filling the page with soft lines, with the shadows below his eyes and the texture of his curls.

I thought about what Beth had said: that I should draw what I felt. I tried to think what I felt about Kit. I couldn't see him the way I had even a day ago. The face on the page had laugh lines and a soft mouth. I could feel his skin as I drew. I could feel the dip in his upper lip, the hard angle of his jaw.

"Come on, let me see," Kit said.

"No, I'm not finished."

"Let me see what you've got so far."

"Nope." I slapped shut the sketch pad and tossed it over the seat.

"Why? Did you screw up already?"

"No! I just don't want you to see it yet."

"That sounds like you screwed up."

"Stop." I kicked at him but he caught my foot and held it still. I could feel his fingertips sinking into my bones. I felt happy suddenly. In spite of everything – the girl, and Jamie and Beth, and what might happen next – here in the car I was happy, with Kit's hand on my foot and the strange, bleak desert coming to light, holding its breath all around us.

"When will we get there?" I asked.

Kit shook his head. "I don't know. It's a big place. Everything is far away."

Finally, when the sun was bright in the sky and we'd

driven through the hills, both starving, we saw the sign for Kilmore. It wasn't really a town – more like a few roads that dumped into the highway, with clusters of buildings on either side, a couple of gas stations, a diner, and a low-slung concrete motel with a giant neon cactus looming over it.

"Hey," I said, "isn't this where we stopped before?"

Kit nodded, looking around. "Yeah, where we ate on the way down."

"This is where you got the beer."

The corner of his mouth jerked down. "Yeah."

The diner was on our side of the road with lorries in the parking lot, three of them, huge, silver, and vaguely menacing. Kit pulled off the highway and parked.

"Okay," he said, letting go of my foot. "Do your thing."

I looked at him. "Thanks for driving me."

He smiled. "Not like I had anything better to do."

"I know, but still. You didn't even complain that much."

I took my sketch pad and started to get out of the car, but he caught my shoulder. He pulled me toward him, sliding his arms around me, his mouth on mine. Inside the world of that kiss, I couldn't think about anything.

Kit cupped my face in his hands. He held it so gently that it made me feel like something fragile and small, a bird's nest or a piece of glass.

"I like kissing you," he said.

I looked straight into his eyes. "I like kissing you, too."

It was only later that I thought about the words: "I like kissing you," not "I like you."

It was almost seven o'clock, and the diner was busy, with waitresses skirting past each other around the square tables, lingering to laugh at something one of the truckers said. And it seemed to be mostly truckers, or at least men wearing trucker hats and T-shirts, their arms brown from the sun. They glanced up curiously when we came in, then went back to the vigorous clatter of their breakfasts, scraping forks across their plates, sucking down long drafts of coffee.

"Hey," Kit said. "That's the girl who served us before."

The pretty Mexican girl, the one he and Jamie had practiced their Spanish on, was carrying a tray of dirty dishes back to the kitchen.

We sat near one of the windows, which was cracked open a few inches, overlooking the dusty parking lot. The landscape was different here. There were more shrubs and pockets of trees, and striated red bluffs rose in the distance. We'd passed long lengths of barbed-wire fence, with cattle grazing behind them.

The smell of gasoline wafted in from the pumps. There were two yellow paper menus, stained and wrinkled, stuffed between a napkin holder and a large bottle of ketchup.

The Mexican girl came over with a pen and said haltingly, "Yes? What can I get?"

"Hola, guapa," Kit said expansively, flashing a big smile at her. "Remember me?"

She smiled back, nodding and checking the door. *"Hay otro?* The other boy?" Her voice had a soft, exotic trill.

So she did remember. It was only three days ago.

"No," I said. "He's not with us."

Kit kept smiling at her. "Yeah, all you've got is me this time. Think you can handle it?"

I couldn't believe he was doing this in front of me. I frowned at him, but the waitress was already laughing, her face opening up. "Okay. What can I get?"

I said quickly, "Actually, do you mind if we ask you something? The day we were here, Saturday, did you happen to see this girl?" I fumbled through the sketch pad while Kit sighed. "Did she come here for breakfast or lunch maybe?"

The waitress looked confused. *"Otra vez?"* she said, turning to Kit. "I don't understand."

I held the drawing out to her, and her face changed. She looked from me to Kit, then abruptly left the table.

"Well, that was smooth," Kit said. "Nice job. She didn't even take our order."

"She would have had our order ten minutes ago if you weren't so busy hitting on her," I snapped.

"Oh, give me a break. I wasn't hitting on her."

"Right. You would have acted exactly the same if she were a guy."

"Sure."

151

I rolled my eyes at him. "Maybe you really are gay."

He started to react, then just laughed at me. He lifted my hand from the table and ran his fingers lightly over my forearm. I shivered.

"Cut it out," I said, pulling away. "Look, somebody else is coming."

An older woman with short gray hair strode briskly to the table. "Elena says you have a question?"

I nodded, holding out the sketch. "We were just wondering if this girl had been here. If you'd seen her in the last few days?"

"Why are you asking?" the woman said coldly.

Kit wasn't going to help. He sat back, watching me struggle to explain.

I looked at the girl's face on the page, the dark curtain of hair and the huge, staring eyes. I took a deep breath and began. "There was a car accident, and this girl, well, she's dead. Not from the accident – she was already dead – but we found her. And we're just trying to help the police," I sat up a little straighter, "help the police identify her and figure out what happened."

The woman's expression didn't change. "The police have already been here. We told them everything we know."

I swallowed. "Well ... do you mind telling us? Have you seen her?"

The woman paused. "There's nothing to tell," she said finally. "The girl was here on Saturday, but she came in alone and left alone."

"Really?" I clutched the pad. It was the first time I'd been able to picture her alive. I imagined her walking through the door, her long hair swinging. "Did you talk to her? Did she say where she was from? Where she was going?"

The woman's mouth clamped down in a line. "I told you, that's all we know. And don't bother Elena anymore about this, do you understand? She's not involved."

I shot Kit a quick glance. What did that mean? He flattened the menu and then folded it, saying easily, "Listen, that's okay, we won't bother anybody. But isn't that a little strange? You know, that she came in alone. And left by herself. It's not like this place is exactly a ..." he hesitated, "tourist attraction."

The woman took the menu from him and slotted it into the space next to the napkin holder. "I don't think it's so strange. We see all kinds of people come through here. We don't know anything about them."

"But if she didn't have a car—" I began.

The woman turned to me, suddenly impatient. "She was a hitchhiker, that's my guess. Truckers pick them up all the time. She got a ride in and a ride out. Did you two order yet?"

"No," Kit said sheepishly, and took out the menu again. I could see Elena hovering near the door to the kitchen, her brown eyes darting toward us.

As soon as the woman left, I leaned across the table, whispering to Kit. "So she *was* here! I knew we'd find out something."

"Yeah, exactly what the police found out. Big deal."

"But she was in this restaurant! She could have been sitting right at this table. Somebody must have seen something. Don't you think? I mean, I wonder which waitress took her order."

Kit looked at Elena. She was busily wiping the counter, her arm moving in quick circles. "I think it's pretty obvious," he said.

I shook my head. "Elena? But then why wouldn't she just say so? What's the big secret?"

He was still watching her. "She's probably illegal," he said.

I stared at him.

He shrugged. "Think about it. Her English isn't good. She's young. And the owner, if that was the owner, doesn't want her talking to anybody about the dead girl. Especially not the police."

"But then—" I leaned across the table. "Then we have to talk to her! Maybe she knows something and she hasn't told the police."

Kit shook his head. "Do you think we could order breakfast first?"

"Okay, okay. But I'm not even hungry anymore."

"Well, I am."

So I sat back, frustrated, and we ordered breakfast, but I mostly just pushed the eggs around on my plate and watched Elena. She served and cleared our table, shooting little smiles at Kit but not really responding to his comments.

"We have to get her to talk to us somehow," I said when she finally brought the check.

Kit dug a few bills out of his wallet. "Wait here," he said.

I watched him catch her arm as she was about to disappear into the kitchen. He leaned against the wall, smiling down at her, and she blushed, resting the tray against the counter so she could free one hand to give him change. But when she fumbled in her skirt pocket, he shook his head, stopping her hand with his.

It made my throat tighten. But at the same time, I could see it was working. She was listening to him, shy but interested, glancing around nervously. Kit dipped his head and kept talking. She bit her lip and looked at her watch, considering something. Then the gray-haired woman came out of the kitchen right behind them and they both jumped. Elena lifted the tray from the counter, gave Kit a quick glance and a nod, and hurried past him.

Kit sauntered back to the table looking pleased with himself.

"What happened?" I asked.

"She'll meet us outside on her break. At ten."

"She will? That's great! Then we can talk to her."

"Listen, let me handle it, okay? You're too ... intense about it. She's not going to talk to you."

"What do you mean?"

"You'll scare her off. You have to take it easy."

"But I can do that," I said.

155

He smiled at me. "No, you can't." He took my fingers and lifted them to his face, rubbing them against his cheek.

"You need to shave," I said.

"Yeah, well, somebody didn't give me time this morning."

Just then his cell phone rang, a long shrill *burrrrr* that I hadn't heard in days. For a few seconds neither of us even recognized it. Then Kit dropped my hand – dropped it the way you drop spare change on a table – and searched his pockets.

"Hello? Hey, Jamie. What's up?"

I tensed.

"Yeah, sorry about that. We're in Kilmore."

Kit shifted in his chair and widened his eyes at me.

"You know, it was Luce's idea. Talk to her about it."

I took the phone and held it close to my ear. "Jamie?"

His voice was rushed. "Luce, what the hell are you doing? Why'd you leave? Mom is going to go crazy when she finds out you're not here. And what about Dad? You guys need to come back. Now."

"No," I said carefully.

"What do you mean, no? You took the frigging car! What's going on?"

I swallowed. "We're trying to find out what happened to the girl. And Jamie, guess what? We're at that place where we stopped on the way down, remember? Where you and Kit spoke Spanish to the waitress? And it turns out the girl was here, too! On Saturday."

Jamie's voice was impatient. "Then you should call the police and tell them. But you need to come back. What the hell is Kit doing driving you all over the state? How'd you ever get him to do that?" I could hear the bewilderment in his voice. I thought of last night on the floor of the study.

"We'll come back soon," I promised. "Don't tell Mom. It'll only be a couple of days. You can cover."

"Cover? Are you kidding? What am I supposed to say?"

I felt a sharp prick of anger. "Say whatever you were going to say to her. Tell her the real reason we're staying."

"Luce." He sounded surprised. Hurt.

"Listen, just let us see what we can find out, okay?"

"Put Kit back on."

"We have to go," I said. "Bye." I clicked off the phone and handed it to Kit. "We should keep it off. Because we're in a restaurant."

He nodded, his mouth twitching. "Yeah, the restaurant. He's pretty pissed."

"Well, so what? I'm mad at him, too."

"At least we've got cell reception again," Kit said. "It's like we're back in civilization."

We both stared out the window, at the sandy parking lot, the sad little clump of buildings, and the thin road forging across the dry land.

"What do we do now?" I asked.

"Wait till ten," Kit said.

25

At ten o'clock, we saw Elena get her purse from behind the counter and fumble for a pack of cigarettes. She slung the bag over her shoulder, glanced once in our direction, then walked out the rear door of the diner.

After a minute, Kit and I followed her. She walked around to the side of the building, a long blank wall with a rusty air conditioning unit jutting out from the center. Elena set her purse on top of it and boosted herself up. She watched us come toward her.

"Smoke?" she asked Kit, shaking a cigarette out of the pack. He took one, then her lighter, expertly flicking it so the blue flame flared between them. They lowered their heads together. I stood to the side, waiting.

Elena pulled a pretty flowered comb out of her hair and shook her hair free over her shoulders. She smiled at

Kit. "So … *qué pasa*? What do you want to know?" she said in her soft voice.

Kit leaned against the air conditioner. "Whatever you can remember about the girl," he said, smiling back at her. "You said she was here on Saturday. Was she with anyone?"

Elena shook her head. "No. *Sola*. I talk to her a little."

"You did?" I stepped closer, I couldn't help it. "What did she say?"

Kit frowned at me, but Elena turned. "She want a ride."

"Where to?"

Elena tapped the cigarette on the metal edge of the unit, sending a shower of ashes into the dust. "Albuquerque."

Kit blew a cloud of smoke into the air. "Did she get one?"

Elena looked from Kit to me and nodded slowly. *"Sí."*

Kit leaned closer, almost touching her. "Whatever you can remember," he said. "It would help, you know? We won't tell anyone."

"The man with the blue truck," she said. "He take her."

"What man?" I asked. "Was it someone you know?"

Again, she nodded, almost imperceptibly. I could see the muscles in her cheek tighten. She turned the wooden comb over in her hands and looked at it.

"Elena," Kit said. "Who is he? What's his name?"

"No sé," she said. "I don't know his name."

I bounced impatiently on my toes. "But he's come here before? Does he live around here?"

She glanced at her watch and slid off the air conditioner, dropping her cigarette in the dirt. She crushed it under her shoe and turned to Kit. "He come here all the time. Every day. He has a blue truck," she said again.

"Thanks," Kit said. He touched her shoulder. "Thanks for telling us."

She looked at him uncertainly, then walked back toward the door of the diner.

"Well, that was weird," I said to Kit.

He shrugged. "I don't know. She doesn't speak much English. Maybe it just seemed weird because of that."

"But it sounded like she knew the guy."

He nodded. "Or at least recognized him."

We started walking back to the car. Kit took out his phone and clicked it back on. "Let's see what Jamie had to say, huh?" he said. He listened to the messages, grinning, and I could hear the faint sound of Jamie's voice, sharp and insistent.

"Come on," I said, tugging his sleeve. "We don't have time for that. We have to think what to do."

"What do you mean? We're done. We'll call the police and tell them it was a guy in a blue truck. Let them figure out who it was."

Kit opened the car door for me and I slid inside, yelping at the hot vinyl of the seat.

"We can't do that," I said. "They'll ask how we know, and you said yourself that Elena won't talk to them. Not if she's here illegally."

Kit looked down at me. "Luce, come on. There's nothing we can do. How are we going to find some guy with a blue truck? There must be a million guys with blue trucks. And here's the other thing: What do we do when we find him? I don't get this. I don't get what you want."

"I want to know what happened to the girl," I said softly.

"We know what happened to her. She died."

"But—" How could I explain it? "Kit, listen. There's more. I know it. If this guy lives around here, if he comes to this place every day, well, we can—"

Kit banged the top of the car. "We can what? I mean, jeez, Luce, what are you thinking we can do? Find this guy and rough him up? Get some information out of him? He's just some guy. He didn't do anything."

I looked at him. "He left her there."

"But you heard what the police said. She was already dead. You're acting like it's murder."

I sucked in my breath, pressing my sketch pad against my chest. "No," I said. "Not murder. But it's something. He left her there."

"She was already dead," Kit said again.

I stared at him, and despite the heat, I felt a cold prickle under my skin.

Just then the phone rang. "Oh, here we go. Jamie's on the warpath," Kit said, bringing it quickly to his ear. "Hey, man." I saw his face change, and he turned away, shielding the phone with one hand. "Oh, *hey*. Hey, Lara."

Lara Fitzpatrick. I stared at him. What was Lara Fitzpatrick doing calling his cell phone?

Lara was the social secretary for the Westview Student Council. Pretty, smart, nice. Nice even to freshmen. Ginny and I had interviewed her for the school newspaper last month about plans for the Sadie Hawkins dance, and afterward she said, "You should come, you should come! Ask a sophomore or junior. Those freshmen guys aren't good enough for you."

I watched him walk away from the car. Why was she calling? And why was his voice like that? Eager, completely different. His back was to me. "I thought you were in Chicago. Oh. Really? Oh, okay. Yeah, sorry about that. We didn't have cell service, so I haven't checked my messages. How are you?" He kept walking, almost out of earshot. He cupped the phone against his cheek. "I've been thinking about you."

I watched his back moving away from me. He ran his fingers through his hair while he talked.

"I know, me too. Me too."

His voice was softer, I couldn't hear what he was saying. I got out of the car.

"Yeah, we were supposed to be. But we kind of had an accident. No, I'm fine, nothing like that. It was an animal or something. But we thought – well, it's kind of a long story." He walked across the parking lot, telling her what happened. I followed him.

"So, anyway, that's why we're still here. Actually, we're

in a place called Kilmore now. I got stuck driving Luce up here, you know, Jamie's sister. Yeah." He laughed. "Yeah, she is."

I was what? My stomach clenched. I stood silently behind him, staring at the tilt of his head, the relaxed curve of his shoulders.

His voice had a tenderness to it, something I hadn't heard before. "Well, it's no fun without you. I miss you."

So this was it. Kit and Lara Fitzpatrick. How could I have been so stupid? How could I have thought he liked me?

He cradled the phone with both hands. "I *really* miss you. I think about you all the time."

I thought of him kissing me, the first time on the porch, the time on the road. And then the other times, at Beth's, in the car this morning. I couldn't stand there and listen anymore. I walked directly in front of him and snatched the phone away from his face. He jerked back, eyes wide, and I saw everything chasing across them, a flash of surprise, then protest, then a kind of regret. "Luce," he said.

I could hear Lara's voice. "Kit? Kit?"

I lifted the phone. "His name is Frederick," I said.

I clicked it off and threw it back at him, straight at his chest. His hands came up to catch it, and I walked away before he could say anything.

26

I didn't turn to see if he was following me. I walked as fast as I could. Past the shining sides of the big trucks, past the diner, past the car. I walked back the way we came, on the shoulder of the road, into the basin of land. It was stupid, of course. There was nothing in that direction. I should have gone toward town, but I wasn't thinking, and by the time I realized it, I couldn't turn around. I had to get as far away from Kit as possible.

It hadn't meant anything to him. None of it. Why did I think it would? He was the same person he'd always been, and the only thing surprising about the phone call was that the girl was Lara Fitzpatrick, who was much too nice to end up with Kit.

But if she was his girlfriend, why had he never mentioned her? On the way down, he and Jamie had talked about one girl after another, but I didn't remember ever hearing him say her name. Although I hadn't really been listening. On Saturday, I didn't care. It seemed so long ago. I'd just assumed he wasn't seeing anybody. But a guy like Kit was always seeing somebody.

It was hot on the road. Little waves of heat rose in the distance and made the asphalt shimmer like a river. I could feel the sun beating on my scalp, slicing through my hair like a red-hot blade.

I heard a car behind me. I glanced over my shoulder in time to see Kit swerve across the road, slowing down next to me, the car's tires scattering the gravel.

His arm hung out the side and he brushed his fingers over the door. "So that was a nice move," he said. "Telling her my real name."

I kept walking, not looking at him.

"Come on, Luce. Don't be mad." He drove alongside me. "I mean, what did you expect? You didn't think we were going to..." Don't say it, I thought. Don't make it worse.

"You didn't think we were going to go out, did you?" His voice was full of amazement. "You're a *freshman*. You're Jamie's sister, for chrissake."

He reached out to touch my arm, but I jerked away and stepped off the shoulder, onto the hard red ground.

"Hey, where are you going?" he called. "There's nothing out here. You should have walked the other way, you know." I could hear the smile in his voice and it just made me madder. I started to run.

The car rolled after me. "So, what? You're never going to talk to me again? Come on. Will you just get in the car?"

In the distance, I saw a car coming toward us. A horn blared.

Kit sighed. "Are you going to get in the car or not?"

I didn't answer. The other car was getting closer, honking repeatedly.

"You know what? I'm not doing this. You're on your own." Kit accelerated off the shoulder and back into the right lane, the tires spitting stones at my shins just as the other car roared by. I watched him pull ahead of me and turn around, heading back toward town.

I kept walking. I lifted my hair off my neck with one hand, tugging my shirt away from my skin. High above, the sky was blue and cloudless. Sometimes a huge semi thundered by, and once a truck driver honked at me, raising his hand out the window as he passed. But then it was quiet again. No cars, no houses, no people. Just a few cattle, moving far away in the field.

Up close, I could see that this place wasn't empty at all. It was cluttered with boulders, little gray-green bushes, the occasional brittle, twisted trunk of a tree. Lizards streaked across the sand, darting under rocks. Birds flitted from bush to bush, chirping raucously. Something rustled behind a boulder and I saw a thin tail lash the ground.

166

I walked on. The mindlessness of it was soothing somehow. I was so hot and tired I couldn't even think about Kit. Sweat trickled down my cheeks and ran into the neckline of my shirt. I tucked my hair behind my ears. My throat was dry. My eyes ached from the glare on the road.

Finally I stopped. I hunched over my knees for a minute, resting. I might as well turn around. It was a long walk back to Kilmore.

I heard the distant sound of an engine and looked up. Far away, coming toward me, I could see a car ... no, a truck. But not a big one, some kind of pickup. I squinted. It was blue.

A blue truck.

My breath caught in my throat. Okay, I thought. There must be a lot of blue trucks.

But she said he lived around here. She said he came to the diner every day.

I looked behind me. The road was deserted. All around me, dry grasses hummed and whispered. I was alone.

The truck was getting closer. There wasn't time to do anything. I stepped off the road onto the sand. This is stupid, I thought. It's just somebody going to Kilmore.

But the truck was slowing down.

It braked noisily and pulled onto the shoulder about twenty yards ahead of me, its metal grillwork flashing in the sun. My heart thumped in my chest. I could see the dark silhouette of the driver, but not his face. I stood still,

167

watching. I didn't know what to do. It was too late to run away or hide. I squeezed my hands into fists and waited.

The driver's door swung open. "You need a ride?"

The voice was flat but oddly high-pitched, like it should have belonged to someone smaller than the man who got out of the truck. He was tall and heavy, with short graying hair and a black net trucker's hat shadowing his face. I couldn't see his eyes.

"Where you going?" He stood next to the truck, one hand resting on the door.

I swallowed. "I was just walking."

I watched his hand slide off the door, casual but deliberate. He took a step toward me. "Too hot for walking."

"It's not so bad," I said quickly. The banging of my heart filled my ears. I stepped backward.

He glanced behind him, then squinted over my shoulder. "What are you doing out here?"

"Just walking," I said again. "I'm ... I'm turning around now anyway."

"Going back to Kilmore?"

I nodded.

"That's where I'm heading. I'll give you a ride." He gestured toward the truck and I stepped backward, not knowing what to do.

"No, that's okay. I'd rather walk."

He was close to me now, a few arm's lengths away. I looked up into his face and his eyes were small and pale, a milky blue. I could hear the low, steady rumble of the truck's engine. He smiled, but the smile never reached his eyes. "Come on," he said. "Don't you want a ride?"

Suddenly, I saw the girl's face, wet with the rain. *Help me,* I thought.

And then the man's expression changed. He frowned, looking past me. I turned and saw a car coming, small in the distance but getting larger, a familiar bronze color that almost matched the dirt.

Kit.

"That's my boyfriend," I said quickly, turning away from him. I started to run, my feet pounding the gravel, half expecting him to come after me, even though I knew that he wouldn't, not with Kit there.

"Kit!" I yelled, waving my arms. "Kit!"

Kit slowed down in the opposite lane and rolled down his window. "Are you talking to me now?"

I ran across the road, lunged at the passenger door and grabbed the handle.

Kit was looking at the man. "Hey," he said.

"How you doing?" the man said in his flat voice. "It's too hot for her to be walking. You can't do that around here when the weather's like this. People get heatstroke, you know. Die from it."

"Really?" Kit looked over at me, scanning my face, his eyes questioning. "I'll tell her to be more careful." He shrugged. "But it's not like she listens to me."

"They never do," the man said, his mouth twisting. He walked back to the truck.

Kit turned to me. "You okay?"

I nodded, blinking back tears. My arms were shaking so hard I had to press them against my stomach to hold them still.

"What happened?" His voice was worried. "Did that guy do something?"

I shook my head.

The truck pulled back into the road, and the man looked straight at me as he drove by. His pale eyes showed no expression at all.

"Huh," Kit said. "Blue truck."

27

"It was him, it was him, it was him." I rocked back and forth in the seat, hugging myself.

Kit put his hand on my shoulder. I flinched, not wanting him to touch me, but at the same time wanting it more than anything. The weight of his hand steadied me. I tried to stop shaking.

"Hey," he said. "It's okay. What happened back there?"

I swallowed. "He asked me if I wanted a ride."

"Well, it's hot out."

I looked at him. "It wasn't like that. He wanted me to get in the truck." I shivered, and Kit slid his hand down my arm, cupping his fingers under my elbow.

"Luce," he said gently. "Maybe he was just offering you a ride. You heard what he said. People get heatstroke."

"No. It wasn't like that."

"How do you know?"

I took his hand off my arm and sat straighter, willing myself to be still. "I could feel it."

Kit didn't say anything for a minute. "Everybody has a pickup truck around here. There must be plenty of blue ones."

I turned in the seat to look at him. "Kit, it was him. I *know* it."

Kit kept his eyes on the road. He let out a long breath and then nodded slowly. "Okay," he said. "Okay." He put his hand on my shoulder again, rubbing his fingers over the back of my neck.

"You can't do that," I said, shrugging free. "I mean it."

He took his hand away, but the imprint of it tingled.

"So what do you want to do?" he said. "Call the police?"

I bit my lip. "What would we say?"

We were nearing Kilmore again, passing the diner. I jolted forward. The blue truck was parked in front. "Look! He's right there." I turned to Kit. "Quick, pull in."

Kit veered into the parking lot and slowed the car. "Okay, Luce. Now what?" He looked over at me, shaking his head. "Suppose it is the guy. How are you ever going to prove that? Do you think you can just walk up and ask him?"

I pulled my feet onto the seat and rested my face against

172

my knees. He was right. How could we prove anything? And what had the guy done, anyway? He'd left the girl on the road, but she was already dead. Was that even a crime? It had to be.

I remembered his voice: *Don't you want a ride?* Is that what he'd said to her, too?

I rubbed my forehead. "Listen, I know it's him. We just need some reason for the police to … you know … question him." I stared at the blue truck. If the girl had ridden in it, maybe she'd left something behind. "Let's look in his truck."

Kit raised his eyebrows. "Look for what?"

"I don't know."

"Just walk over there and search his truck?"

"Yeah."

"That is a really dumb idea. And probably illegal."

I frowned at him. "Then you should be happy. Didn't you say everything fun is illegal?"

"Okay, well, I was wrong. Because that is not fun, and probably illegal, and totally pointless."

I kept looking at the truck. She'd been inside it, I knew it. Maybe it was the last place she'd been alive. "I'm going to do it."

"Go ahead."

"Are you coming?"

"No."

I got out of the car and slammed the door. The diner windows faced the gas pumps at an angle. You could see this part of the parking lot from the corner tables, but not easily. I shielded my eyes with one hand and tried to see who was sitting there. But the sun was too bright. The windows reflected the image of the road, the motel on the other side, the giant cactus.

I walked toward the blue truck. Part of me couldn't believe I was doing this. What if it was locked? But no, when I tried the handle, the passenger door opened easily. I looked around to make sure no one was watching, then climbed inside.

The cab had a stale, old-food smell. The carpet was dark with stains and littered with junk: two beer bottles, a crumpled Coke can, a half-empty bag of potato chips. I kept checking the door of the diner. No one went in or out. The parking lot was quiet, baking in the sun.

I got up on my knees and peered between the seats: a ballpoint pen, some change, a folded newspaper. I flipped down the visors. A pair of sunglasses.

What was I looking for? I didn't even know. Some sign the girl had been here, sitting on this very seat the day she died. But it was all so ordinary. This was the kind of stuff in anybody's car.

I opened the glove compartment and took out the sheaf of papers inside. Car stuff mostly, the manual for the truck, an insurance card. An insurance card. It had his name on it. And an address. *Wesley Wicker, R.R. #7, 4420 Brick Road, Castle, NM.*

"Hi." I heard Kit's voice in the parking lot, sounding

unusually loud. I jerked around and saw the man – the man! – coming out of the diner. I ducked down in the seat and tried to shove the papers back into the glove compartment, my fingers fumbling and almost dropping them.

"Did you see my friend in there?" Kit said. "I lost her again."

Holding my breath, I pushed the door open, an inch at a time. I squeezed out, crouching next to the truck.

"Nope, didn't see her." A short nasal laugh. "You better keep an eye on that one." As quietly as I could, I pressed the door shut.

"Yeah, well, thanks anyway."

Still crouching, I ran in front of the two other cars and around the corner of the building. *Wicker, 7, 4420, Brick, Castle,* I kept whispering to myself.

I stood with my back against the wall, breathing hard. A minute later, Kit rounded the corner, swearing.

"Sorry," I said miserably.

"Are we done now? Because, you know what, that guy is creepy as hell and I'd just as soon not run into him again."

"I got his address," I said.

"That's great. You can send him a card. Can we leave?"

"I want to go to his house."

Kit grabbed my shoulders and pulled me away from the wall. "No way! No! Luce, listen to me. We're not going to his house. I don't know what his deal is. Maybe he's the guy who dumped that girl, maybe he's not. But there's something weird about him. We're not doing it."

I slid out from under his hands and started to walk back to the car. "Listen, you're right, I have to be more careful," I said. "I shouldn't have looked in his truck like that, not when he could walk out and see me."

I stopped to wait for him, but he was still standing there scowling. "Kit, please. Listen a second. The police didn't find any ID on her, remember? No purse, no wallet. So somebody probably took it. Somebody *stole* it. And if that guy was the last person with her – the last person to see her alive – maybe he's the one."

"Maybe he is. And guess what? Maybe we'll never know."

I nodded slowly. "But we have to try to find out. At least, I do."

"Why?"

I walked back and stood in front of him, looking into his eyes. "I don't know. I just do."

He stared down at me, his forehead creased with frustration. Then his face changed, and in a careful way, he took a strand of my hair and tucked it behind my ear. "I don't get why this is so important to you."

I turned away. "Well, I don't get why it was so important for you to kiss me if you were going out with Lara Fitzpatrick."

"I wasn't the only one doing the kissing. If you remember."

"I'm trying not to."

I walked toward the car, then hesitated, my fingers on the handle. "So will you take me? To his house, I mean?"

Kit opened the door and climbed inside. He sat with his hands on the steering wheel, looking out at the dusty lot. "What if it's locked?"

"It won't be," I said. "The truck wasn't."

"You didn't find anything in the truck."

"No."

"What makes you think you'll find something in the house?"

I didn't answer. I watched his profile. His jaw tensed, softened, tensed again.

"If we go to his house, that's it," he said. "Whatever happens. If we find something, we tell the police. If we don't, the whole thing stops. Okay? We go back to Beth's."

"Okay," I said.

"I mean it."

"I said okay."

I lifted my sketch pad from the back seat and tore out a page. Across the top I wrote *Wicker, R.R. #7, 4420 Brick Road, Castle, NM.*

28

"So where are we going?" Kit asked.

"The town is called Castle," I said. I fished the map out of the side pocket of the door and spread it across my lap. This part of the state was an empty yellow square crossed by a half dozen thin lines, the only roads. Castle had to be near one of those. I squinted at the town names. Tucumcari. Conchas. Mosquero. It might have been a foreign country.

"Here it is," I told Kit. "East of here. About twenty miles."

We turned onto another highway. Kilmore disappeared behind us. The flamboyant cactus sign looked cheap and brittle in the distance. We passed a trailer with laundry hanging limply from a clothesline. We passed a house with a weathered chicken coop and four gray hens scratching the dry ground.

"Do you think this is still Kilmore?" I asked.

"Yeah," Kit said. "The suburbs."

Then we were surrounded by nothing.

It didn't take much time to cover twenty miles, especially compared with the long drive that morning. Soon we were approaching a gas station. The sign said "Castle Gas and Service."

"What's the name of the road?" Kit asked, pulling up to the pumps. A stooped old man in blue coveralls came out of the tiny building and walked over to Kit's window.

"Could you fill it up with unleaded?" Kit said. "And we're looking for a road—" He turned to me.

"Brick Road," I said. "And it says something else. R.R. 7. Do you know what that means?"

The man shuffled to the pump, ignoring me. When he came back to the window he tugged on his bottom lip, showing a crooked jumble of yellow teeth. "Rural Route 7. Brick Road. Same thing. It's the next right."

"Thanks," Kit said, paying him.

"It's not paved," he called as we drove away.

The next right was miles farther along, and it turned out to be a bumpy dirt track winding down a slope.

Kit shook his head. "Look at this place. Castle. Where's the castle? Where's the frigging run-down shack? There's nothing here."

"The house number is 4420."

"Something tells me you can't miss it," Kit said.

We jolted over the road, churning up clouds of dust.

"What if he was on his way home?" Kit asked. "He left the diner. He could be there right now."

"Yeah," I said, staring at my lap.

There was a house up ahead, a trailer. I leaned forward. "There, look, that's it." But it wasn't; it was 4460. "So we're close." I glanced at Kit. His brow furrowed in annoyance.

We passed three more houses in a little pocket, then another dull stretch of road. Far away, on a rise, I could see a white house flanked by outbuildings: a shed, some kind of garage. "That's it," I said. No blue truck. A metal mailbox leaned crookedly on a pole, with the numbers 4420 on it. Kit pulled onto the dirt driveway.

Kit shut off the engine and we sat for a minute, looking around.

"See, there's no sign of him," I said.

"Oh yeah? You're sure of that? What about the garage?"

I shook my head. "It's just got some kind of machinery in it. He's not here."

"Okay, but we're not staying long. Do you understand?"

"Stop treating me like I'm six years old," I snapped at him.

"I will, when you start showing more sense than that."

We climbed the steps to the front door. I reached for the knob, but Kit stopped me. "You'd better knock," he said. "What if somebody else is here?"

I hadn't even thought of that. What if he didn't live alone? And then what would we say? "We'll ask for directions," Kit said, before I could open my mouth.

"You sound like you've done this before," I said. I knocked on the door. We waited, listening to the silence.

"Okay," Kit said. "I'll park behind that shed. In case he comes back. And listen: no messing around. We're in and out of this place. If we can even get in." He walked back to the car, calling over his shoulder, "Is it open?"

I tried the doorknob. It was locked.

"Yeah," I lied. "Just give me a second." I scanned the front of the house. The windows were all closed. Now what? I heard Kit start the car as I jumped off the porch and ran around to the side, breathing a sigh of relief when I saw a small window cracked four or five inches. It was above a propane tank, so I had something to climb on. I scrambled on top of the tank and pushed up the screen, opening the window all the way. Inside was a bathroom with soap-scummed blue tile.

I squeezed through the window, scraping my ribs against the frame and half climbing, half falling onto the toilet seat. Then I ran to open the front door.

"So it *was* locked," Kit said smugly.

I didn't say anything.

He looked at his watch. "You've got fifteen minutes. That's all. Then we're leaving."

"That may not be enough time."

181

"It'll have to be. He could be on his way back. So get moving."

I surveyed the house. It was small and messy, but strangely impersonal. There were no pictures on the walls, nothing on the coffee table but old newspapers and a half-filled drinking glass. The living room was cluttered with big, ugly furniture, a sofa and armchair covered in rust-colored velour. A crumpled T-shirt lay on the floor, a pair of wadded-up socks beneath the footstool.

"Don't touch anything," Kit said.

"I'm not stupid, you know."

"Thirteen minutes," Kit said.

"Help me, then," I said. "You look, too."

"What are we looking for?"

I shrugged helplessly. "I don't know. A purse or a wallet, credit cards. Something of hers. Look in the kitchen. I'll check in the back."

I walked down the dark hallway. I could hear Kit in the kitchen, drawers scraping and rattling. It was a tiny house, not much bigger than an apartment. There were two bedrooms, but one was filled with junk: an old fan, luggage, cardboard boxes, the kind of stuff you put in a basement. The other one was his. The bed was unmade, a clump of sheets, with the bottom sheet pulled loose from the mattress. There were dirty clothes in a pile on the floor, an empty bag of chips on the nightstand. I tiptoed through the mess, looking around. I knelt on the floor and peered under the bed. A shoe, a magazine. I pulled open the drawers of the long bureau and cringingly felt through their contents, trying not to disturb anything.

Kit appeared in the doorway, shooting a quick glance out the bedroom window. "Six minutes," he said. "See anything?"

I shook my head. "Did you find anything in the kitchen?"

"Nope. All his stuff, nothing with a girl's name on it. He's a mechanic." Kit held out a small white card. "Has his own business."

"Put that back," I said, pulling away. "And can you check the storage room? Maybe he hid something in there." I closed the bottom drawer of the dresser. Only the closet was left.

I looked outside again; still no sign of anything. The road was empty. Pushing open the closet door, I scanned the rack of hangers. Jeans. Plaid shirts. A sweatshirt. Who was this guy? It was impossible to tell. It felt so odd being in his house, such an invasion of his private world. Except this world didn't seem private at all. Just blank and impersonal.

The shelf was too high for me to see what was on it. I reached up and groped along the edge. It was creepy, going through his things like this. I imagined his pale eyes watching me. I shivered. More clothes, a sweater. Then something hard.

I stopped. Stretching as high on my toes as I could, I pushed my fingers further onto the shelf.

There it was. A hard corner. It felt like a box.

"Kit," I called. "Come here. There's a box, but I can't reach it."

He came to the doorway, looking nervous. "Yeah? What is it? Time's up. We have to go."

"Help me get it down."

Kit reached up easily and grabbed it. A brown shoe box. He set it on the mattress. We looked at each other. "It's probably just some shoes," he said.

"Yeah." I sat down, lifting the lid.

It wasn't shoes.

It was a bright clutter of objects. At first it made no sense. A gold button. A dangling earring studded with turquoise. A purple barrette. Little things. Girl things. The kind you lose or leave behind. It made me feel strange, sorting through them. In fact, it felt stranger and stranger, like they weren't forgotten things at all. They were things that had been taken.

On purpose.

I froze, looking at Kit.

"What the hell ... ?" he said.

Two more earrings, without matches. I touched them, brushing them aside. A pretty decorated hair comb, wooden, with flowers painted on it. "This looks like what that waitress, Elena, had in her hair, doesn't it?" I asked softly.

Kit frowned, taking it from me. "Yeah, it does," he said.

I felt like we'd stumbled into the cave of an animal. A secret nest scattered with bones and fur, the remnants of lives.

Then I saw it. A tiny silver shoe, covered in red sparkles.

I picked it up, staring at it. It dangled from a broken link.

"Shit," Kit said.

29

I dropped it as if it were on fire. The charm clinked when it fell, hitting an earring.

"It's hers," I whispered.

"Maybe not," Kit said.

"Kit, it's hers! It's from the bracelet. Remember the other charms? They had links just like this."

He nodded slowly, running his fingers through the jumble in the box. He picked up a small plastic vial. "What's this?"

It was a medicine bottle, unmarked, half-filled with pinkish-white tablets. I took it from him and unscrewed the cap.

"Aspirin?" I asked.

Kit shook his head. "We need to get out of here."

His fingers closed over my hand. "Luce, we shouldn't

even be touching this stuff. If this guy is some kind of pervert, I mean, if he did something to these girls, and that's how he got their stuff ... well, this might be evidence or something. And we've put our fingerprints all over it."

I pulled my fist free and dumped a pill into my palm, slipping it into the pocket of my jeans. "I know. You're right. But we can take this to the police. Maybe it's cocaine."

Kit just looked at me. "You think *that's* cocaine? A pill?"

"Well, something else then. Something illegal." I stared at the box again. "This is the guy, Kit. I know it. He did something to her. We've got to call the police. When they see the charm, they'll know—"

And then I stopped. The police didn't know about the charm bracelet. They didn't know because I'd taken it off the girl before they'd had a chance to see it.

The charm would mean nothing to the police.

I turned to Kit. "The bracelet," I said. "They don't know about the bracelet."

He looked at me, a long steady look, and took the bottle and cap from my hands.

"Oh, God," I said.

"Luce." When I lifted my head, he was watching me with an expression in his eyes I didn't recognize. "It'll be okay," he said. "But we have to go. Now."

I stood numbly by the bed, barely able to nod.

Kit screwed the cap back on the bottle, wiped it on his

T-shirt, and dropped it in the box. Then he set the lid on the box and carefully put it back on the shelf, arranging the pile of clothes to cover it. "Is that right? Is that how it looked?"

I knew he needed me to answer. I took a deep breath. "Yeah."

"Luce, come on. We have to get out of here."

He tugged me away from the bed, and then there were things to do. It was good to have things to do. We moved quickly through the house, making sure it looked just the way it had when we came in. I let Kit out the front door and bolted it, then went back to the bathroom to climb through the window. Once I'd squeezed through, breathless and aching from the pressure on my ribs, I squatted on top of the propane tank. I slid the window back to its original position, then replaced the screen. Kit rounded the corner of the house. "What's taking you so long? Come on!"

"Okay, I'm done," I said.

We ran across the yard and scrambled into the car, flooring it out of the drive. A fog of dust rose in our wake, blocking the house from view.

30

We sped up the dirt lane toward the main road.

"We'd better not run into him here," Kit said. "I mean, the guy's a freak. And he knows what our car looks like."

I twisted to face him. "Kit, what are we going to do? The charm – it's the thing that proves he was with her. It proves he left her there."

Kit shook his head. "Not without the bracelet."

"But what can we ... how can we explain it to the police?"

"I don't know."

We bumped onto the highway, heading back the way we had come. I looked out the window. I thought of him leaving her here, in the middle of this vastness, where he knew no one would see him.

"He can't get away with it," I said.

Kit stared straight ahead. "We don't even know what he did."

"We do," I said. "We do know. You saw the stuff in that box. Those things didn't belong to him. Kit, he took that charm from her, like some kind of sick souvenir."

"Like you took her bracelet."

"No!" I cried, stung. "No, it wasn't like that."

He glanced at me. "Listen, I can't think about it now. Let's just get away from here."

"Okay. We'll go back to Kilmore. We can stay there tonight. We know he goes to that diner."

Kit shook his head. "We should go back to Beth's and call the police."

"And tell them what? That we broke into some guy's house and found a box full of junk that proves he was with the girl? It won't mean anything to them. Kit, please. Can't we stay in Kilmore?"

"At that motel? What's the point?"

I was silent.

"It'll cost money."

I shrugged at him. "We were going to stay at the hotel in Albuquerque anyway. This is no different."

"That was on the way to Phoenix! That was part of the plan."

"Well, the plan changed. Kit, please. Just give me a chance to figure out what we should do."

"Yeah, you're great at that. You're full of brilliant ideas."

I stared at the hard line of his jaw. "Stop."

He looked at me, quiet.

Then I remembered the pill. I dug it out of my pocket and turned it over in my palm. It was large and circular, with the letters PAX on one side. "It says P-A-X on it," I told Kit, holding it out for him to see. "Have you ever heard of that?"

He glanced at the pill but didn't say anything.

"Well? Have you?"

"It's E," he said finally, his eyes on the road.

"E?"

"Ecstasy."

"Oh." I knew about ecstasy, a little, from the drug awareness talk at freshman orientation. "But that's, like, a party drug, isn't it?"

"Yeah."

"Why would he have a bottle of that?" I didn't understand.

Kit was quiet for a minute. "Didn't Mrs. Corell talk to you guys about that stuff?"

Mrs. Corell was the Health Ed teacher. Everybody made fun of her droning lectures on sex, alcohol, and drugs because they were full of oddly specific instructions for the many ways Westview students could screw up their lives.

"Yeah, I guess," I said. "But I forget. What does it do again?"

"It's a sex drug," Kit said flatly.

I stared at him. "You mean, like, date rape?"

He shrugged, his face grim. "Maybe."

"So all that junk in the box ... Wicker must have..." I stopped, thinking of the girl. And the other girls. "Can it kill you?"

He shook his head. "I don't think so."

"But, Kit, there was something wrong with her heart, remember? Beth said she had congenital heart disease. Do you think he gave her the pill and it caused a heart attack?"

"I don't know."

I shuddered, rubbing my arms. "Kit, if he gave her that pill and it killed her ... that's murder."

Kit said nothing, staring straight ahead at the long, gray ribbon of road.

31

It was mid-afternoon by the time we got to Kilmore. Kit parked at the motel with the neon cactus, the Desert Inn. The parking lot was empty except for a station wagon and a minivan. When we walked into the small front lobby, a bored-looking guy not much older than we were said, "Yeah? Can I help you?"

"We need a room," Kit said, "just for one night."

"Two beds," I added quickly.

The guy scratched his neck and took a key from the rack behind him, sliding it across the counter. "Here you go. It faces the pool. You got a credit card?"

The pool turned out to be a small turquoise rectangle enclosed in chain-link fencing, with a narrow diving board at one end and scuffed plastic deck chairs scattered along the edge. Kit eyed it as we walked past.

"We could swim," he said.

"Now?" I looked at him in amazement.

"Why not? It's hot enough." He stopped in front of a blue metal door and pushed the key into the lock. The room, cramped and ugly, made me wince. It had two double beds, tan carpeting spotted with stains, and a laminated, fake wood nightstand with a lamp on it. The bedspreads and drapes looked shabby. A large, garishly colored mountain scene, drenched in orange and purple, hung on one wall.

"Christ," Kit said. "Now do you want to swim?"

"I want to figure out what we should do. I want to talk."

He nodded, looking around. "We can talk at the pool."

I sighed. The room was depressing, and suddenly I *did* want to swim, to do something normal and mindless for a change. "Okay."

We'd brought our swimsuits because my dad's condo complex in Phoenix had a pool. I took my backpack into the bathroom with me and closed the door, slipping off my flip-flops and standing nervously on the cold tile until I heard Kit cross the room and start rustling in his own bag. I stared at my face in the mirror over the sink. In the harsh fluorescent light, it looked different to me. Sharp and serious, bruised by shadows. The skin under my eyes had violet smudges. It had been days since I'd really slept.

I stripped and pulled on my swimsuit, wrapping the thin, white bath towel around my waist and knotting it.

When I opened the door, Kit was sitting on the edge of one bed in his swim trunks. He watched me walk across the room. I pulled the towel tighter around me.

"Cut it out," I said.

"Oh, relax."

We were the only ones at the pool. The white concrete deck blazed in the sun, scorching my feet. I hesitated at the edge, but Kit ran past me, soaring laterally through the air and diving into the water. I secretly wanted him to look awkward, but his dive was smooth and graceful. His body knew exactly what to do.

The splash sent a cold spray over me and I jumped back. He burst through the surface, shaking hair out of his eyes and laughing. "Wooo-hoooo! Come on, get in."

I lowered one foot into the water, and the shock of the temperature made my toes curl. "It's too cold!"

"No, it feels good. Dive in."

I crouched on the edge, leaning over the water. I dipped my fingers in it. I thought about the girl, how the rain streamed over her face. "Kit, what if that guy—"

Kit shook his head firmly, swimming toward me. "Don't think about it. Let's just forget about it for a while."

We can't, I wanted to say. A girl is dead, and we've found the guy who did something to her. But I looked at Kit's shining wet face, at the hopeful expression in his eyes. I felt tired of it, too, overwhelmed.

"Dive in," he said again.

I shook my head. "I don't know how to dive."

Kit raised his eyebrows. "You're kidding."

"No, I really don't. I'm not a good swimmer."

"Then jump in."

I sighed, dropping my towel on the concrete. I took a deep breath and jumped in.

The cold water hit me like a slap, rushing over me and making my heart seize. My feet hit the bottom, and I came shooting back to the surface. The chlorine burned my eyes. "Oh!" I gasped. "It *is* cold."

"Move around." Kit swam closer, grinning. "You'll warm up."

I shivered in the water, kicking over to the side.

"So how come you don't know how to dive?"

"Nobody taught me. My parents don't swim much."

"Jamie's a good swimmer."

"Yeah. Jamie's good at most things."

Kit was treading water a few feet away. "Does that bug you?"

"No." I shook my head quickly. "I like it that he's good at things. I mean, I'm good at things, too."

"Such as?"

I frowned at him, because of course I couldn't think of anything right then. "Well ... drawing," I said finally.

Kit swam closer, his hands moving easily through the water, cupping and circling, trailing pretty streamers of turquoise light. "Yeah, drawing. You're good at drawing."

196

A nervous warmth crept through me, like blushing on the inside.

"And something else," he said. His face was so close I could see the tiny drops of water beading along his eyelashes and brows. They sparkled in the sun.

"What?"

He smiled at me.

My pulse quickened. I remembered the feel of his mouth, the taste of it. I pushed backward, widening the channel of water between us. "Not as good as Lara," I said, trying to make my voice cold.

But Kit just grinned at me. "Well, Lara. She's a lot more experienced. But you'll get there. With practice."

He glided over to me. Suddenly I was backed up against the wall of the pool, and he was close enough to put his arms on either side of me, his palms resting on the edge.

"Kit," I said.

"What?"

"Don't."

"Why?" He lifted his hand to my cheek, sliding his fingers into my wet hair, moving my face closer to his.

I started to say something – I don't even know what – but then his mouth covered mine, sharp with the taste of chlorine, but gentle, even slow. His arm circled my back, pulling me tight against him, against the hard, damp wall of his chest. I couldn't help it. I wrapped my arms around his neck and kissed him back, breathing him in, touching his shoulders. His lips moved against my cheek. "Luce. Take a deep breath."

And then his mouth was back on mine, firm against it, and we were sliding under the surface in a whoosh. The water was everywhere – cold and quiet – a dense underwater soundlessness that filled my ears, lifted my hair, cushioned us in a silent bubble. It felt like we were trapped inside one of those plastic snow globes, suspended in a place without sight or sound, with the storm whirling all around us.

All I could feel was his mouth against mine. Then he pulled us back up to the surface. When I felt the warm air on my face, I was dizzy and breathless. I pushed away from him.

"What are you doing?" I said, panting for breath.

"Kissing underwater." He grinned at me. "Chick trick."

I stared at him. I felt my cheeks flush, a rising tide of shame. Of course that's what it was. That's what everything was: a chick trick. The little jokes and compliments, the way he touched my hair or rubbed the back of my neck. I thought of Wicker and the girl. What trick had he used to get her into his truck?

"Well, stop it. I don't like that," I said. "Save it for Lara." I swam across the pool, feeling his eyes on me.

He swam after me lazily, stretching and turning in the water. "You seemed to like it. And why are you so hung up on Lara?"

"Because she's your girlfriend, you jerk." I shot him a

quick, uncertain glance. "Unless you're planning to break up with her."

He snorted. "Break up with her? Why would I do that? We're going to the prom in a month."

Of course. I climbed onto the edge of the pool and huddled there.

He swam closer. "What's the matter?"

I couldn't look at him. "I don't get it. Why are you ... why are you doing this with me? What would Lara say if she knew?"

Kit shrugged. He was treading water a few feet away. "She doesn't know. And anyway, it's no big deal."

I felt my stomach clench and curl into itself. "Nothing's a big deal to you."

"Well, jeez, Luce. *Everything's* a big deal to you."

We glared at each other.

"Not everything," I said finally. "But this ... I mean, it's like ... it's like you're just using me."

Kit's eyes flashed. He swam to the edge, his hand on the concrete near my ankle. "Is that what you think?" I could hear the sharpness in his voice.

I nodded, staring at my knees.

"Hey, it wasn't my idea to drive to Kilmore. It wasn't my idea to search some pervert's house. It wasn't my idea to pay for a room at this frigging motel! If anyone's getting used, it's me."

I scooted away from him. "That's not true."

"No? Think about it."

He splashed out of the water, heaving himself onto the deck and running past me to the diving board. He bounced hard, launching deftly into the pool. When he surfaced right in front of me, he flipped his hair back and stared up at me.

"So now what?" he said.

I didn't answer.

"Oh, okay. You're not talking to me again?"

I swung my hair over my shoulder and gathered the dark length of it, squeezing out the water. "Look, I can't do this anymore. I wouldn't have done it at all if I'd known…" I stopped, embarrassed.

"Luce." His voice was gentle in a way I didn't expect. When I looked up, his eyes were on me, green and gold in the sun.

"Did you really think I wasn't seeing anybody?"

I didn't answer.

"Luce, you're a freshman. Did you really think you and I—"

"No," I said quickly. "Stop. Let's not talk about it anymore."

He sighed, pushing back from the wall. He swam to the rickety metal ladder near the diving board. I watched him climb out. His shoulders were freckled from the sun.

He saw me watching him and smiled suddenly, an easy, rueful smile that seemed to apologize and forgive at the same time. "Okay, let's forget it."

I studied him doubtfully.

"Don't be mad," he said. "I won't try anything else, I promise."

I rubbed the towel over my arms, feeling hollow. "Okay."

"Don't dry off yet. I'm going to teach you how to dive."

I shook my head. "No way."

"Oh, come on."

"Uh-uh."

"Why not?"

"I'm really bad. I don't go into the water at the right angle."

"You can't be that bad."

"I am. Believe me."

"Try it."

I sighed and walked to the diving board, aware of him watching me the whole time.

"Watch how I do it," he said.

He jumped twice on the end of the diving board, and it made that low springy noise, full of anticipation and promise. Then he arced through the air and sliced the water, barely making a splash.

He bobbed to the surface, grinning.

"Okay," I said. "Just so you know, when I dive, it won't look anything like that."

"Show me."

I stepped onto the board and walked carefully to the end. I put my hands together in front of me, pressed my face between my arms and jumped over the water, trying to turn my body in the air so my head went in first. But I didn't make it. I hit the surface with a loud smack.

"Owww! Owww!" I yelled. "See! That's what I told you. Ow. It kills."

Kit was laughing. "That was really bad," he said. "Oh my God, you weren't kidding. You're terrible."

"Thanks."

"It's okay, I'll teach you." He swam over to me.

"You can't teach me. That's what I'm telling you. It's hopeless."

"Not regular dives like that. I'll teach you some fancy ones."

"What are you talking about? If I can't do a normal dive, there's no way I can do something complicated."

"Sure you can. Watch." He swam to the edge of the pool and climbed out, running ahead of me to the diving board.

"Cannonball!" he yelled, bouncing hard on the end and flinging himself into space. He gripped his knees, tucked his head under, and landed with a huge splash, dousing me with water.

When he burst through the surface, I laughed at him. "Anybody can do that."

"No. No way," he said, mock serious. "The form is very tricky. Try it."

I ran to the end of the board and jumped far over the pool. I clutched my knees, pressing my forehead to them, suspended for a minute in the warm, clean air. Then I plummeted into the water.

When I came up, laughing and spluttering, Kit was already on the pool deck. "Hammerhead," he called, running to the end of the board and throwing himself in a tight ball into the water, headfirst. He burst through the surface. "Whooo!" he cried.

So that was the afternoon. They weren't dives, they were jumps. There were some I remembered from the public pool when I was little: watermelon, jackknife, can opener. But Kit knew dozens of them. My favorite was the squirrel, a kind of reverse cannonball with your hands gripping your ankles.

Finally, after what seemed like hours, I climbed onto the deck and lay flat on my towel, squinting up at the cloudless sky. "I can't do anymore," I said, laughing. "My stomach hurts."

"See," Kit said. He lay down beside me. "You can dive."

I held my stomach. "Ow-ow-ow," I moaned. "That's not diving. Anybody can do that."

"Hey, you had great technique for the squirrel."

I looked over at him, shading my eyes. "Yeah, well … I had a good teacher."

He smiled at me.

I turned away. "So who taught you all of those?" I asked.

He was quiet for a minute. "My dad."

"Really?"

"Yeah. He's not a great swimmer, but he loves the water. He's always showing off."

I thought of Kit's dad, sneaking into bars with other women, getting Kit in trouble with his mom. He didn't sound like the kind of person who would teach his son twenty different ways to dive. I looked over at Kit. You could never guess what people were really like, inside.

We lay there with the hot sun on our faces. In the distance, I could hear the faint, sporadic drone of cars on the highway. I wondered where the blue truck was now.

32

"I have an idea," I said.

We were lying on the beds in the motel room. It was almost dark outside. Kit had gotten two sodas from the vending machine by the pool, and he was holding one against his forehead – he had a chlorine headache, he said – while I rolled mine across the bedspread, playing with it.

"You won't be able to open it if you do that," he said. "It'll explode."

"I know, but listen," I said. "The bracelet. What if the police could find the bracelet somewhere?"

"What do you mean?"

I reached for the strap of my backpack, pulled the bag over to the bed, and felt inside. I held the bracelet up for Kit to see, dangling it from my fingers. The charms nestled against each other. "What if the police could find the bracelet with Wicker's stuff?"

"Huh?"

"If they find the bracelet with his stuff somehow, and then they search his house and find the charm ... well ... it's a connection."

"You're nuts," Kit said.

"No, think about it."

"I don't have to think about it. It doesn't make sense. As far as the police are concerned, the bracelet has nothing to do with the girl."

"But if they found it in his house—"

"Luce, whether they find the bracelet in his house or in a frigging ditch, it's not going to make any difference."

I sighed, rubbing my forehead. "Well, what do you think we should do?"

"I don't know. I really don't. But I'm hungry. Let's see if the diner's still open."

A loose string of cars and trucks lined one side of the parking lot. As we crossed the highway, Kit stopped short.

"Damn," he said.

"What?"

"Look." He pointed.

I gasped. The blue truck. "What's he doing here?"

"Who knows. Maybe he's here 24/7. Stay away from him this time, okay?"

Kit started forward but I stayed where I was, biting my lip. "I forgot my soda," I said.

Kit turned to me. "So? You can order one."

"No, that's a waste. I'll just run back and get it."

"You're going back for your soda?" He looked at me incredulously.

"Yeah. Give me the room key." I held out my hand.

He frowned. "Hurry up," he said, throwing it at me. "I'm hungry."

I jogged back across the road and around the side of the motel to our room. My mind was racing. The truck. I could put the bracelet in the truck. The girl had been in the truck, I knew she had. There must be some evidence of that. And if the police found the bracelet in his truck, that would be their first clue.

I pushed open the door and snatched the bracelet from my backpack, shoving it in my pocket. I almost forgot the can of soda, but then I grabbed that, too.

33

I stood in the dark parking lot, my heart pounding. I could see the people through the diner windows: a waitress leaning over a table, a man throwing back his head and laughing. I couldn't see Kit. I couldn't see Wicker. There was no sign of anyone outside. The blue pickup was parked at an angle, slightly away from the other cars and the two big trucks. What if it was locked? It hadn't been before.

I steadied myself and walked over to it. I kept my eyes on the door of the diner. It stayed shut. With one hand, cautiously, I tried the passenger handle. It lifted easily and the door swung open. The overhead light in the cab flashed on, and I reached up quickly to flip it off. I set the can of soda on the ground and carefully, tremblingly, tugged the bracelet out of my pocket. I crouched next to the passenger foot well and hesitated. If I hid it in the litter of bottles and wrappers, he might find it. Or worse yet, gather it up with all the other junk and throw it out by mistake.

I kept shooting glances at the diner. Should I put it between the seats? Under one of the seats? Gingerly, I reached my left hand under the passenger seat. My fingers swept over a crinkly mess: more paper, a bottle, the hard handle of something. I stood up slowly and cradled the bracelet in my palm. I looked at the charms again: the hourglass, the treasure chest, the horseshoe, the heart. I thought of how easy it had been to unclasp the bracelet and slip it out from under the girl's arm. It was the only thing left from that night. After a minute, I pushed it deep beneath the seat, into that tangled, sharp-edged darkness.

I looked again at the entrance to the diner. There was no sign of anyone. I flipped the overhead light back on and quietly closed the door to the truck, nudging it with my hip till it clicked. But then, as I turned, I tripped over my can of soda. It rattled on the rocks, a low rumble of noise that seemed to echo and magnify in the stillness. For a minute I was groping frantically in the dark. Then I felt the cool side of the can and clutched it against my chest. I crossed the parking lot, and went into the diner.

Kit was sitting in a booth under one of the windows, talking on his cell phone. I could see him smiling into it and hear the charge in his voice, the coaxing, generous pauses. It was Lara. Obviously. He glanced up at me. His eyes were vaguely challenging.

"Sure," he said into the phone. "Definitely. Sorry about before. Yeah, well, nobody calls me that, I don't know why she said it." He made a face at me. "I'll talk to you tomorrow." His voice softened. "You too. Bye."

I slid into the booth, setting the soda can between us, not saying anything.

"What took you so long?" Kit said. He nodded his head in the direction of the bar. I saw Wicker sitting at one end, hunched over a plate of food, just a guy in a nondescript plaid shirt and jeans. His pale eyes flickered toward me, then away.

"Where were you?" Kit said again. "I already ordered."

I paused. "I couldn't get the door to the room open," I said. I was going to tell him about the bracelet, but not now, not with Wicker watching us.

He frowned. "What'd you do? Get another key?"

"No," I mumbled. "I finally got it open." I picked up the menu and pretended to study it. "What'd you get?"

"A burger. Fries."

The older woman came to the table, the one who'd taken our order that morning. I asked for a hamburger and a milk shake. She scribbled it on her pad, looking at us curiously but not saying anything.

"I thought you wanted your soda," Kit said.

I looked at the can. "I changed my mind." I leaned forward, lowering my voice. "So what's he doing?"

Kit bent so close I felt his breath on my cheek. He whispered, "Eating."

"Come on, be serious."

"Well, what do you think he's doing? He's having dinner. Pretty suspicious. I mean, what does he think this is, a restaurant?"

"Stop."

He leaned back, smirking.

When the food came, we ate in silence. The waitress ripped the check off her pad and left it on the table. I wanted to look at Wicker, but I could feel his gaze on me and it gave me chills.

"Is he watching us?" I asked Kit.

Kit glanced at him and frowned slightly. "Yeah. But not us. You."

I cupped the cold milk-shake glass in both hands and huddled in the corner of the booth. "Tell me when he leaves."

"He's leaving now. He just paid. Okay, don't freak, but he's coming over here."

I stiffened, but before I could even react, Wicker was standing at our table, looking down at me. His eyes flitted over my face. They had the same flat quality I'd noticed before, as cold as metal. I swallowed.

"You're not from around here, are you?" he said.

"No," I said. My voice sounded high and uncertain.

"So where you from?"

I hesitated. "Kansas."

He laughed, a short, nasal burst, and I saw his Adam's apple bob and jerk, so that the untanned part of his chest was exposed, just for a second, above the collar of his shirt. "Kansas! What are you doing all the way out here?"

"We're just driving through," Kit said. "Crossing to Arizona."

"Huh." He kept looking at me. I couldn't drag my eyes away. "Be careful. This place isn't like Kansas."

I nodded mutely. And then, as suddenly as he came, he was gone. The diner door slammed behind him, and we watched him through the window as he drifted across the dark parking lot toward his truck, shoulders hunched, head down.

I set my milk shake on the table, unable to drink the rest. "I put the bracelet in his truck."

Kit stared at me. "What?"

"I put it in his truck, under the front seat," I said.

"You're not serious."

"Listen, Kit. It'll prove she was there. We can call the police and—"

"What do you mean you— Wait. That's what you were doing? Getting the bracelet?"

"Yes. I put it in his truck. Kit, if we don't do something, no one will ever know. They'll never catch this guy. And it's not just the girl! There were others. You saw what was in that box. And someone like Elena, you said yourself she can't go to the police. The bracelet, it'll prove the girl was in his truck."

"What the hell do you think you're doing?" Kit

pushed violently back from the table, banging hard against the booth. "Listen to me: It doesn't prove anything."

"But—"

"I keep telling you. *The police don't know the bracelet belongs to the girl.* For that charm to mean anything, they'd have to find the bracelet with *her,* not him. Don't you see?"

"But—"

"Besides, you don't know whether that girl was ever even in his truck. You don't know."

"But she was! Kit, I know it."

"Look, you may think that, but it's not up to you. You can't just decide the guy is guilty, and then, like, plant evidence in his truck. I mean, who do you think you are, the goddamn judge and jury?"

He glared at me.

"But—"

"But what? You can't just make this stuff up as you go along."

I shrank back from him. "I wanted to fix it," I said miserably. "I just ... I can't stand for him to get away with it."

"Get away with what? We don't even know if he did anything!" Kit yanked his wallet out of his jeans and tossed a twenty on the table. "Shit," he said, standing up.

"Wait," I pleaded.

He picked up the soda can and banged it against the edge of the table, gripping it tight. "Now we have nothing. We can't even show the bracelet to the cops and tell them what happened. They'll never find it now. They have no reason to search that guy's truck. And even if they did, the bracelet could belong to anyone—his girl-friend, his daughter, anyone."

I felt a surge of shame.

"You're right," I said.

"Yeah. Now you tell me."

He turned and strode to the door. I scrambled out of the booth and followed him.

"Kit, wait." I ran after him, grabbing his sleeve.

"No," he said. "Go back to the motel. You've got the key."

"What are you going to do?"

"What do you think I'm going to do? Get the bracelet back."

"But how?"

He barely looked at me, jerking free and walking toward the highway. "I know where he lives."

"I'll go with you."

"No."

"But you don't know where I hid it."

"Under the seat. I can find it."

"Kit." My fingers circled his arm. "I'm sorry," I said. "I'm really sorry. Let me go with you."

He shook free and kept walking. I ran after him. "You need someone to read the map."

"No, I don't. I know how to get there."

"Kit, please."

We stood there, at the edge of the parking lot, separated from the motel by a moat of pavement. The neon cactus flickered urgently above us, full of its own bright, false assurance. Kit gave me a long, angry look.

But then he shrugged, and when he crossed the road in the darkness, I was right beside him.

34

It was hard to see the turnoff. We drove past the gas station, a low fortress of concrete, and I kept my face to the window, peering desperately into the black night. The moon was a weak sliver.

"Here it is," I said quickly, seeing a break in the right side of the road.

Kit turned sharply, grinding gravel.

"Slow down," I said. "It's too loud."

The rumble of the car on the rough road was deafening. He glanced at me.

"How will we ever get close enough to his house without him hearing us?" I asked.

"We'll do it," Kit said. But his voice was grim. We reached a hummock in the road and suddenly we could see his house.

Our car slowed to a crawl, but still I could hear every crunch of stone. "He's going to hear us," I whispered.

"He may not even be home," Kit said.

But as we came closer to his driveway, I could see the truck. A light was on in the front window.

"Okay," Kit said. He pulled off the road and killed the engine, turning off the headlights. We sat in the quiet car, looking at the house. The yellow light from the front window shone steadily into the yard. I couldn't see anyone inside.

Kit put his hand on the door handle.

"No," I said. "Let me go."

"Uh-uh, wait here. It won't take long."

"Kit, you don't know where to look."

"I can find it."

I touched his arm. "Let me go. It'll be faster."

He looked at me doubtfully, then back at the house. "Okay," he said finally. "Be careful. And hurry."

I opened the door as quietly as possible and slid my foot onto the road. I was still wearing my flip-flops. Not good for running. I got out, still watching the house. I gently swung the car door closed, my hands trembling, but didn't latch it. Then I started across the yard toward the dark shape of the truck.

As I got closer to the house, I could see the window was open. I heard the faint drone of the TV, voices interspersed with canned laughter. The front door was still. My heart was pounding, my blood beating in my ears.

Silently I crept to the passenger side of the truck and felt in the dark for the handle.

Still no sign of movement from the house. I lifted the handle and slowly opened the door. It made a low, groaning noise, and the light flashed on, flooding the cab. Panicking and blinking against the sudden brightness, I scrambled onto the seat and flipped it off. I crouched there, frozen, my eyes fixed on the house. But the TV voices continued, and nobody came to the window.

Okay, I thought, hurry, hurry, hurry. I shoved my hand under the seat, groping. Paper crinkled beneath my nervous fingers. I felt that hard handle of something and pushed it away. Where was the bracelet? I reached farther, leaning over the foot well, my arm almost entirely under the seat. I knew where it should be. Here on the side. But maybe when he was driving, maybe on the rough road, it had rolled and tangled itself somewhere else. I stretched my fingers flat and ran my palm desperately over the wreckage beneath the seat.

Then I felt something small and smooth. One of the charms, I was sure of it. I curled my fingers around it and tugged. Immediately the bracelet sprung free. Its chain swung against my skin.

"What do you think you're doing?"

The high, nasal voice came out of the darkness right next to me, and as quickly as I sprang back, out of the truck, it wasn't fast enough.

He was standing there, staring at me, his face a mask.

218

I couldn't speak, couldn't swallow, couldn't breathe. I turned to run, but his hand shot out and grabbed my arm. His grip was as tight as a vice.

"What have you got there?" he asked, edging between me and the passenger seat, his eyes flicking down to my hand.

I tried to hide it, spooling the metal links into my fist. But not before he saw it. Even in the darkness, I could sense his eyes focusing on it.

"It's hers," he said finally. I felt a cold blade of fear slice through me. "Where'd you get it?"

I couldn't answer. He shook me suddenly, a sharp jerk that almost knocked me to my knees. I cried out and stumbled back to my feet, his hand still locked on my arm. "Tell me," he said. "Where'd you get it?"

I shook my head, gulping. But then he squeezed my arm so hard I yelped, and he brought his face close to mine. I could smell him, a cold, sour smell. I cowered. "What are you doing out here?" he said. "Where's your boyfriend?"

He ducked suddenly and shoved one hand beneath the passenger seat. When he brought it out again, it held something small and thin. Something with a handle. I couldn't see it, and then I could. A knife.

"Please," I said, my voice strange and shaky, not my voice at all. "Please."

And then I heard a sound. A hissing sound, close to us. Wicker turned, lifting the knife, and I squinted into the darkness. Something silver came flying toward us.

"Run, Luce! Now!" I felt wet drops spitting over me and heard a dull crunching sound as the soda can smacked the left side of Wicker's face. He let go of my arm, staggering backward.

I ran. Blindly across the hard ground, through the rough grass, straight into the night. When I tripped in my flip-flops, I kicked them off, and the rough stones stabbed my bare feet. I could hear Kit behind me, and then Wicker's grunt and cry. "Hey!" But we were at the car, scrambling inside, and Kit was fumbling with the keys, shoving them into the ignition.

"He's coming, he's coming, he's coming," I sobbed, watching the darkness shift, both shielding and revealing whatever was out there.

The engine roared, the tires spun on the gravel, and Kit turned the wheel sharply. We veered off the road for a minute, making the turn, and then Kit gunned the engine and sped back toward the highway.

He didn't look at me. He was leaning over the wheel, his eyes locked on the road. "Is he following us? Can you see the truck?"

"No," I whispered. "No, not yet, but Kit, hurry. Hurry."

The road disappeared behind us. I couldn't see the house. The car jolted onto the smooth surface of the highway, and I huddled in the dark, the bracelet clutched in my hand.

35

"We have to call someone," I whispered, barely able to speak. I kept looking behind us. No headlights.

Kit nodded and tossed me his cell phone. The panel of turquoise light beamed brightly in the darkness, but I couldn't get a signal.

"Wait till we're closer to Kilmore," Kit said. He kept checking the rearview mirror. Finally he turned to me. "You okay?" he asked.

I nodded mutely.

"Luce? Are you?"

"Yeah," I said, forcing my voice into some semblance of its normal self.

"You should have let me do it."

I nodded again, but I was thinking of what Kit had said about putting the bracelet in Wicker's truck. About me being judge and jury.

"Kit, when he saw the bracelet, he said, 'It's hers.' "

Kit didn't say anything.

"He did this to her."

"Yeah."

Finally the NO SERVICE message on the phone stopped blinking. "I want to call Jamie," I said.

"You should call the police."

"I know, but Jamie first, okay? You have the number at Beth's, right?"

Kit shrugged. "Listen to the messages. It's on there. There must be a dozen from Jamie."

I started to play through the messages, but the first one was from Lara. I stiffened when I heard her voice. "Hey, Kit—"

Kit must have realized who it was, because he reached for the phone. "Here, you don't know how to work it. I'll get the number," he said quietly.

He dialed for me and handed it back. A few seconds later, I heard Beth's anxious voice say, "Hello?"

"Beth, it's Lucy. Can I talk to Jamie?"

"Lucy! Where are you? We thought you'd be back hours ago. What's going on?"

"We found..." I sucked in my breath. "We found the guy, Beth. The one who left her there."

There was silence on the other end of the line, a beat of nothing, then her voice, puzzled, disbelieving. "What do you mean? How do you know?"

"It's a long story. Can you call the police for us?"

"Have them come to the motel," Kit said.

I nodded at him. "Could you tell them to meet us at the Desert Inn in Kilmore? That's where we're staying. And, Beth ... could you tell them to come soon?"

"Lucy," Beth said. "What happened?"

"I can't," I said. My voice was shaking. "There's too much. I'll tell the police. But can I talk to Jamie?"

I heard the hesitation at the other end of the line, then Jamie's worried voice. "Luce? Where are you?"

"Jamie, we found the guy. The one who left her on the road. We think he killed her."

"But it was heart failure," Jamie said.

"I know, I know, that's what the police thought. But we went to his house and we found pills, ecstasy—"

"Ecstasy?" Jamie sounded stunned. "Luce, you have to get back here. Now. Mom and Dad have both called, like, five times today. Asking where you were, who you're with, what's going on."

I sighed. They knew just enough to be worried. "Call the police for us, okay? Right now?" I said finally.

"Okay," Jamie said. "But Luce – are you all right?"

"Yeah," I said. I missed him, suddenly. Missed not just him but myself, who we were four days ago, before any of this happened. I thought of the two of us when we were kids, all the crazy stuff we used to do. And how things turned out fine, more or less, every time.

Jamie sighed. "Man, do I want this to be over."

"Me too," I whispered.

I clicked off the phone and held it in my lap. If it was so hard to explain to Jamie and Beth, how would we ever tell the police?

It was well past midnight when two police cars pulled into the motel lot. We'd been watching the highway, sitting in silence on the edge of Kit's bed. I could feel things changing, the tipping of one reality into another. It reminded me of that moment on the road when we first found her. The rising panic was the same. And the sense that everything was about to be different.

I had the bracelet in my hands. I slid it back and forth between my palms and stared at the tiny charms. I thought of the girl buying each of them, carefully choosing the horseshoe for luck, the treasure chest for its surprising cache of jewels. The bracelet was an intimate record of who she was.

The blue lights of the police cars flashed over Kit's face in a sudden strobe. He looked so serious, almost frightened. The knock on the door made us both jump.

When I opened it, the sheriff was standing there, and the cop with the nice eyes who had questioned me on the night of the accident.

"Miss Martinez?" Sheriff Durrell said. "You remember Sergeant Henderson. I understand you have some information for us."

I nodded, opening the door wider. I held out the bracelet. "I—"

But Kit crossed over to me, grabbing it from my hand. "I took this from the girl," he said, not even looking at me. He gave it to the sheriff. "The night of the accident. It was on her wrist."

I stared at him. So many feelings hurtled through me that I didn't know what to do. And then, suddenly, I did. I reached for Kit's arm, and slid my hand down it till my fingers laced with his. "No," I said. "I took it."

Kit turned to me, but I didn't look at him.

The sheriff watched us. His face was unreadable. "Does one of you want to tell me what's going on?"

And so we did.

We sat on the edge of the bed and told them what had happened. About the bracelet and my sketch of the girl, going to the diner, finding out about the blue truck. The sheriff asked the questions, the sergeant took notes. The part we glided over, not giving the details, was the part about Elena, the waitress. We didn't want to get her in trouble. Kit just said we'd shown the sketch to people at the diner, and one of them had recognized the girl.

"Who?" the sheriff asked sharply. "Who identified her? Did you get the name of the person you spoke to?"

"Um, no," Kit said. "Just some woman."

"What did she look like?" Sergeant Henderson asked.

"I don't really remember," Kit said. "I'm not too good at that."

They looked at me expectantly. I bit my lip. "She had brown hair."

But then we told them the rest of it: meeting Wicker on the road, going to his house, finding the box with the charm and the bottle of pills. I dug the pill out of my pocket and gave it to the sergeant, who squinted at it and handed it to the sheriff.

"It's…" I hesitated.

"I know what it is," the sheriff said curtly. He and the sergeant exchanged glances, not saying anything.

I told them about putting the bracelet in Wicker's truck.

The sheriff stared at me, shaking his head. "And why did you do that?" he asked. "Miss Martinez? Why would you do something like that?"

"I don't know. I thought if you found the bracelet in his truck, and then the charm at his house, maybe you'd … maybe you'd know that the girl had been there."

"I see. So you planted evidence?"

"No, it wasn't like that…" My voice trailed off thinly. It was exactly like that. "I mean, I knew it was wrong. That's why we went all the way to his house to get it back."

I told them everything I could remember about Wicker, his pale eyes, his bristly gray hair.

"You don't seem to have any trouble recalling what *he* looked like," Sheriff Durrell commented.

I swallowed. "I was scared," I said. "He had a knife. I was watching him the whole time."

The sergeant glanced up from his notes. "What kind of knife?"

"I don't know. It wasn't that big, but the blade was long."

"How long?"

I shook my head. "I don't know. I couldn't see."

The sergeant continued writing, his hand moving across the page.

When we finished talking, the room was quiet. The sergeant looked through his notes. The sheriff just watched us, a cold, assessing gaze. He took the pad from the sergeant and flipped through the pages.

"So," he said.

We waited.

"Larceny."

Kit glanced at me.

"Lying to a police officer."

I swallowed.

"Breaking and entering."

The sheriff turned another page.

"Illegal possession of a controlled substance."

He looked at me, and I could only stare at the floor.

"That wasn't ours," Kit said.

"Do you have any idea how much trouble you're in?"

Neither of us said anything. I tightened my fingers over Kit's.

"Do you realize how this information affects the investigation?"

Slowly, I raised my eyes. The sheriff's face was impassive.

"I'm sorry," I whispered.

"Sorry? You're sorry?" He snapped the pad shut with such force the sound made me cringe.

"That girl has been dead for four days. Four *days*. Without identification, maybe with an incorrect finding of the cause of death. You had knowledge, information, an object found on the body of the victim that could have changed that."

My throat ached. I could feel my eyes welling up.

"Listen to me, Miss Martinez. Suppose that girl was your sister. Suppose your sister was found dead on a road somewhere, and the person who found her took information that would have been helpful in identifying her and figuring out what happened to her. Information, in fact, that might show evidence of a crime."

I could feel Kit shift beside me, sitting up straighter. "She said she was sorry," he said.

The sheriff glared at him. "I'd advise you to keep your mouth shut, Mr. Kitson," he said coldly. "I haven't even started with you. You're ... let's see ..." he shuffled through pages, "just four months shy of being legally classified as an adult. Would you care to hear the consequences of these actions for someone over the age of eighteen?"

Kit said nothing.

The sheriff snorted. "I didn't think so."

228

He shook his head and motioned to Sergeant Henderson. "All right," he said to us. "Wait here."

We watched them return to the police car, the bracelet dangling from the sheriff's hand. They sat in full view of the motel window, talking and paging through the notebook.

"Okay," Kit said. "You can let go of my hand now. My fingers are cramping."

"Sorry," I whispered.

He half smiled at me, not his usual smile, but something. I knew he was trying to make me feel better.

It seemed a long time before they came back into the room.

"I'm going to take a ride out to this fellow Wicker's place," the sheriff said. "We'll see what he has to say. Sergeant Henderson will stay here with you." He looked at me sternly. "He'll be in the squad car outside. Neither of you will leave this room. Understand?"

I nodded.

"You'll have to come in to the station for further questioning."

I nodded again.

When they left, the door clicked shut with finality.

36

"Man." Kit let out a long breath. "I'm glad that's over."
He yanked his T-shirt over his head in one swift stroke
and pulled off his jeans. I turned away, but he seemed
oblivious, throwing back the bedspread and sliding
under the sheets. He closed his eyes. "I'm really tired,"
he said.

I sat on the edge of the mattress, twisting my hair. The
small digital clock on the nightstand read 1:00 a.m. "I
don't think I can sleep," I said.

"Well, I can, so turn off the light."

"But what's going to happen now? All that stuff they
said, about—"

"Shhh," he mumbled. "Not now."

"But—"

"Turn off the light."

I frowned at him, but his face was already soft with sleep, his breathing slow. I flipped the light switch and went into the bathroom to brush my teeth. When I came out, Kit was asleep, so I changed into my nightshirt and crawled into the cool envelope of sheets. In the dark, I stared at the ceiling. I was thinking of all the things the sheriff had said, that long list of offenses. I tugged the sheets under my chin. I didn't think I would be able to sleep, but when I closed my eyes, the blankness was a kind of refuge.

I shot upright, shaking all over. For a minute I couldn't even tell where I was, and I whipped around, trying to make out something familiar in the blackness of the room. I'd dreamed about the girl again. This time, as she rose up in the middle of the wet road, she came flying toward me, her sad, dark eyes fixed on mine. I was afraid of her, afraid of what she wanted. I tried to run. Then I woke up.

Kit was still sound asleep, lying on his back, one arm flung over his head. Trembling, I crawled out of bed and groped my way to the bathroom for a drink of water. The white light burned my eyes, but I left it on, with the door cracked, so that the room wouldn't be so dark. The cold water tasted rusty. I carried a glass back to the nightstand and looked down at Kit's calm profile.

I found my sketch pad and took out my pencil. Sitting cross-legged on my bed, I began to sketch. There was just enough light to see his features – nothing sharp or distinct, only the vague contours of his face. I sketched the soft fall of his hair, the line of his forehead and nose. When I got to his eyes, I gently drew the lashes, painstakingly, as if it mattered that I capture every one. Faces looked different in sleep. They became more their true selves, relaxing into their old innocence, without any of the layers of disguise that people wore when they were awake.

Asleep, Kit could have been a saint or an angel. His face was all beautiful lines and curves. He didn't stir the entire time I was drawing him, not even with the harsh light shining from the bathroom. By the time I finished, I knew his face by heart.

I slept so late in the morning that the room was bright when I opened my eyes. The phone was jangling angrily. Kit's bed was empty, and I could hear the whining rush of the shower through the wall. I pushed my hair away from my face and fumbled for the receiver.

"Hello?"

"Miss Martinez?"

I sat up straighter. "Yes?"

"Sheriff Durrell here. We're going to need you and Mr. Kitson to come in to the station and answer some questions."

"Oh. Okay. But ... did you talk to Wicker?"

"We've brought him in for questioning also." I shivered. The "also" made it seem like there was no difference between us, like we were accomplices.

"I don't know where the station is."

"I would have Sergeant Henderson escort you, but I had to call on his services last night."

I looked out the window. The other police car was gone.

"Why? What happened?"

"Miss Martinez." His voice was cold.

"Sorry."

"The station is in Quebrada. It's about twenty miles west of Beth Osway's place. She can direct you."

The shower noise stopped abruptly and the bathroom door swung open. Kit stuck his head out. "Who are you talking to?" he whispered.

"Police," I mouthed. I concentrated on the phone again. "Should we come right now?"

I could hear him pause, thinking. "You can go to Ms. Osway's house for the time being. I'll leave instructions for you. But you need to go there directly. Understand?"

Stupidly, I nodded, then I remembered to say, "Yes, sure, we'll leave now."

"I'll speak with you later today, Miss Martinez."

"Okay."

Kit came out of the bathroom in his jeans, toweling his hair. "So what did he say?"

"They want to talk to us again," I said glumly. "They've got Wicker at the police station."

"Again?" Kit said. "Jesus Christ! We told them everything. I mean, we solved their frigging case for them. What do they want now?"

He looked so outraged, I almost smiled. "I don't think

they see it that way. But they said we can go back to Beth's. They'll call us there. So we need to leave."

He frowned and wadded his clothing into a ball, shoving it back in his duffel bag.

We took a different road back to Beth's, narrower and even less traveled, because we were both sick of that same highway. It looked like a short cut, but it seemed to take longer. Kit called and told them we were coming, and I listened to him avoid Beth's frustrated questions with a vague "Yeah, yeah, we'll tell you when we get there."

I sat with my feet on the dashboard and my sketch pad in my lap, drawing a new line of mountains. These were smaller than the others, gentle rises covered in dark shrubs, nestling close to the road. "Do you think the police will charge us with anything?" I asked.

Kit shook his head. "No way. We didn't do anything wrong."

I glanced at him hopefully. "We didn't?"

"Well, I mean, we did ... but it was for the right reasons, you know? That should make a difference." He sounded like he was trying to convince both of us.

Up ahead, I saw a gas station, and on the side of the road, a hand-painted wooden sign with a woman's face and puffs of smoke all around it. It read "Jinjee, Dream Interpreter – $10/dream."

"Kit!" I said. "Stop!"

"Why? We don't need gas."

234

"No!" We were zooming past it. I grabbed his arm. "For the other thing."

He frowned and braked, turning into the gas-station lot. "What other thing?"

I looked away, embarrassed. "The dream interpreter. I want to talk to her."

"Huh?"

I sighed, finally meeting his gaze. I leaned over the back seat and pointed to the sign. "Look. I've been having the same dream every night since the accident. It's about the girl. I want to know what it means."

"I'll tell you what it means. You were totally freaked out when we found the girl, so now you're dreaming about it. Big deal."

"No, it's more than that. In the dream, she always holds out her hands to me. She wants something from me, but I don't know what it is."

"And you think some kook at a gas station is going to give you the answer?"

"I just want to try it," I said. It sounded pathetic even to me. "I mean, the Indians do dream interpretation, right? It's part of their whole culture. Maybe she can help me figure it out."

Kit ran his hands through his hair, looking annoyed. "Fine, do what you want. I'm getting a soda." He opened the car door.

Inside the small gas-station office, a heavy man in an undershirt was organizing a rack of sunglasses. He looked up when we walked in.

"What can I do for you?" he asked.

"I saw the sign," I said, gesturing.

"Oh, sure. Jinjee. I'll get her for you." He opened a door at the back and yelled. A woman shuffled out, wearing a purple silk robe that was tied at the waist. She had lank jet-black hair hanging on either side of a face that was creased but not wrinkled. I couldn't tell how old she was. She didn't look Indian, more like she might be Chinese.

"Hi," I said awkwardly. "Um, I wanted to have a dream interpreted."

"Okay," she said in choppy English. "Ten dollar."

"Oh." I turned to Kit. "My money's in my backpack. Can you? I'll pay you back." He rolled his eyes and opened his wallet.

"This way," the woman said, opening the back door into a hallway.

I tugged Kit's arm. "You come, too," I said softly.

"Oh, great," Kit muttered.

We walked down the hallway to another door, and when she opened it, we were outside again, in the yard behind the building. There was a makeshift tent a few yards away, with the a cleaned patch of red-brown dirt all around. She strode toward it. Kit and I followed.

"She doesn't even look Indian," Kit whispered. "She's probably just some New Age freak."

"You think it's a scam?" I asked.

He snorted. "Of course it's a scam." He made his voice

somber. "You are going on a long journey. Stay away from the fish."

"Stop," I said. "She's not a fortune-teller."

"Oh, right. Sorry. *Dream interpreter.* That's totally different. That's, like, a science."

I frowned at him. "Look, I want to be able to sleep again. I'm so tired. Maybe she can help."

The tent looked completely fake on the outside, decorated with drawings of stars and flames. But it felt real on the inside. It was dark and stuffy, acrid with the smell of sweat. The woman squatted in the middle, leaving Kit and me to crowd together by the flap.

Kit coughed. "Can I leave this open?" he asked.

"No," the woman said. "No light."

"No air," Kit whispered to me. "It reeks in here."

The woman untied a leather pouch and emptied its contents on the ground in front of her. She sorted feathers, dry flower stalks, a small pile of sand.

"Maybe I should interpret a dream for *her,* " Kit whispered. "I'll tell her I'm having a vision of deodorant."

I elbowed him. "Cut it out," I whispered.

"What's all that junk for?" Kit asked her.

She didn't answer. She started passing her hands back and forth over the piles.

Kit leaned close to my ear. "Oh, God. Here we go."

The woman began to chant, something that was almost a song, off-key. But Kit was right. It didn't sound Indian. Finally she handed me another small pouch. "Shake," she said. I shook it. "More," she said. I shook it again, listening to the dull clatter of whatever was inside. "Now," she gestured for me to dump it out. A bunch of small colored pebbles scattered over the other things she'd arranged.

She studied them without expression and said, "Tell me the dream."

So I told her about the car in the storm, the girl rising out of the road, her arms outstretched, wanting my help. I could see all of it while I talked, as if it were right in front of me: her pale pleading face in the rain.

The woman stared at me. She seemed bored. "She not asking for help. She helping you. She give you something."

"What?" I asked. "What is she giving me?"

The woman shrugged indifferently. "It your dream," she said.

"Well, that was worth the ten bucks," Kit said as we walked back to the car. "Now it's all clear."

I sighed. "Maybe she's right."

Kit shook his head in disbelief. "You're buying that?"

"This whole time, I thought the girl was asking for my help. But maybe she was helping me."

"Oh, yeah? How? By waking you up every night?"

"No." I shook my head. "Helping me see, really see things."

"Like what?"

You, I was thinking. *Jamie. Myself.* But I didn't say anything.

"Oh, come on. That was total b.s. She just threw in the chanting to make it seem spooky. Plus, I hate to break it to you, but she seemed completely bored by your dream."

I nodded. "Yeah, I know. That was bad. I mean, it's like having a therapist be bored by your problems."

Kit laughed. "You should have made something up. Something more interesting. You could have told her a dream about me."

I rolled my eyes. "I don't dream about you."

He slid his hand under my hair, squeezing my shoulder. "Maybe you should. You'd sleep better."

I pulled away, but I couldn't help laughing at him.

Near where we'd parked, I saw a pile of old car parts next to a Dumpster: some shredded tires, a bent muffler, a white-crusted battery. "Hey, look," I said. "Let's take something for Beth."

"Go wild," Kit said, climbing into the car. I thought of the metal pieces in Beth's sculpture. I picked up the rusted muffler and tossed it on the floor of the back seat.

"Kind of like a housewarming gift," I told Kit.

"Freak," he said.

37

It was early afternoon when we pulled off the highway onto Beth's road. The car bumped into the yard, and the dogs came running from the shaded patch by the shed, barking crazily. They stopped, foolishly grinning, when we got out, and circled us, tails lashing our legs. Oscar shoved his head under my hand.

I felt shy suddenly, not wanting to see Beth, thinking of what I'd said to her that night in the kitchen. But it was too late. She and Jamie came out together, hurrying down the porch steps, and their faces seemed to show everything: not just what had happened to them but what had happened to us, and the resulting mix of wonder and panic and worry. When I looked at Jamie, I felt like I was seeing him as a person, separate from me and from our family, for the first time.

"Hey," I said quietly.

"Hey," Jamie said. "You're finally back."

"Are you okay?" Beth was looking at me closely.

"Yeah, we're fine," Kit said. "Just thirsty." He pushed past them into the house, and I ran up the steps after him.

We ended up in the living room, with Kit pacing around, telling what happened, me sitting on the floor interjecting details, and Jamie and Beth on the couch, comfortably part of each other's space. It was hard to explain everything. So much of it had seemed like the only thing to do at the time, but now it seemed like a random bunch of accidents and missteps. It was hard to believe we'd even done these things.

"You broke into his house?" Beth asked in surprise.

"You *took* one of the pills?" Jamie demanded.

And I could only nod, trying to remember our reasons. We were telling them about the knife when the phone rang. I knew from Beth's voice that it was Sheriff Durrell.

"Yes," she said. "Yes, Stan, they're here." She moved slightly away from us, toward the kitchen, but we could hear the murmur from the phone and her concerned "Oh!" and "Really?" in response. Kit looked at me.

"He did?" Beth said. "Wow. Yeah, exactly." There was a long pause, and I could see her back stiffen. "No. No, Stan, please don't. I understand, but..." Now she turned to us, rubbing her forehead, her face pinched. "Stan, you can't do that," she said. "I know. Yes, I know. But they did call you. They told you everything. They're the reason you've got him in custody."

241

What was he saying? What was he going to do to us? Beth waited for a minute more, tense and serious, and then her eyes flickered toward Jamie. "Stan," she said slowly. "Listen to me. They're just kids."

She stared at Jamie and I saw a scrim of sadness fall over her face. She looked older, resigned. "They're just kids," she repeated, gazing at Jamie.

She moved away from us, down the hallway, still talking. After a while, she came back into the room. "Okay. Right. That seems fair. Thanks, Stan. Yes, here she is."

Beth motioned to me, and I stood up slowly, taking the phone, my stomach tight. "Hello?"

"Miss Martinez." The sheriff's voice was brisk. "I'm going to speak to your parents about these latest … developments. Tell Mr. Kitson I'll be contacting his parents as well."

"Okay," I said unhappily. "But please don't scare my mom."

"Miss Martinez, it's not my intention to scare anyone. I'd like to inform your parents of what you've been up to the last few days." He sounded irritated. "Especially since the department is not inclined to bring charges."

I wasn't sure I understood. "You mean you don't have to talk to us again?"

"We have a confession," he said.

"You do?" I felt my knees weakening. I leaned against the wall and slowly sank to the floor. "From Wicker?"

"That's correct."

"What did he say? Please ... what happened to the girl?"

"I can't discuss that with you, Miss Martinez."

"But what did he do to her? Did he drug her? Was that how she died?"

"Miss Martinez," he said curtly. "I can't discuss it."

"Please," I said again.

He sighed. "The full toxicology screen will take a few more weeks, but we're pretty confident about what we'll find."

"Do you know who she is?"

There was a pause. "We have a positive ID. Now I'd like you to put Mr. Kitson on the phone."

I felt a wave of relief. Suddenly, I didn't need to know who she was. It didn't matter. All I'd wanted was to make sure that she wouldn't vanish out here all alone, without anyone knowing, without a name or a home or a family. And now she wouldn't.

Sometimes I'd felt alone like that – like I could disappear and no one would notice. But it wasn't true. There were tiny connections everywhere you looked, ways that lives crossed into each other and changed: me taking the bracelet, Jamie kissing Beth's hand.

I walked slowly across the room and handed the phone to Kit.

Maybe we would never know what happened to her, and maybe that was all right. Not knowing could be a kind of knowing.

When Kit hung up the phone, it was Jamie who spoke, shattering the stillness of the room. "Is it over?" he said, his dark eyes fixed steadily on Beth.

"It's over," she said.

Jamie didn't say anything.

"They have a confession from Wicker," Beth said quietly. "And they're investigating his connection to several other young women."

I looked at Kit, thinking of Elena.

"What happened to the girl?" Kit asked. "Did he tell you?"

She shook her head. "Not much, but a little. They're still waiting on the drug screen, but it sounds like Wicker picked her up at the diner, took her back to his house, and gave her the ecstasy. I guess it causes an increase in heart rate and blood pressure, and she had a reaction immediately because of the defect in her heart. A massive heart attack."

Jamie shook his head. "And then he put her in the truck and just dumped her? On the road like that?"

Nobody answered. We sat in silence, thinking about it.

"So who was she?" Kit asked finally. "Where was she from?"

"He didn't tell me," Beth said. "They haven't reached her family yet." She hesitated. "But you can leave now. You're lucky. They're not pressing charges."

"Yeah, lucky," Kit said, shaking his head. "We can finally start our spring break. Five days late. Jeez." He looked at Beth and Jamie. "Hey, Luce, want to go for a walk? Before we have to get back in the car?"

I knew what he was thinking. To give them time alone.

"Okay," I said. But I was secretly thinking that it gave us time alone, too, and I wasn't sure I wanted that.

I grabbed a bottle of water, and we stepped into the yard. A lizard skittered across the dry ground and under the porch steps, its tail making one final, lateral swish in the dirt. Oscar charged after it, barking and barking, but it was gone.

"Stupid dog," Kit said.

"He's not stupid," I said, snapping my fingers at Oscar. "That's just instinct."

I followed Kit through the brush, hanging behind him, not sure what to talk about. But he wasn't talking. We walked single file through the desert, the mountains like a mirage in the distance. I watched the muscles of his back under his shirt.

After a while he called to me, "Do you think we'll ever find out who she was?"

"I don't know. Maybe when the police finish the investigation."

"We'll be long gone by then."

"Yeah, we'll be home." It felt good to say it. Wandering over this hard, hot land, I thought of Kansas, of the prairie grasses waving in the spring winds.

Kit pointed to the mountains. "Do you think we could walk there? In a day, I mean?"

I shook my head. "They're too far."

"Yeah, you're probably right." He waited for me to catch up, wiping his face on his sleeve. "Man, it's hot."

I unscrewed the cap on the bottle and handed the water to him, watching him take a long swig and then drizzle it over his forehead. "Here," he said, splashing it at me.

"Oooh, it's cold," I cried. I took the bottle and drank, aware that my lips were touching the place where his had been. He watched me.

We were standing in a sandy patch, with tawny clumps of grass scattered around us, little thickets of yellow flowers. "Let's stop for a while," Kit said. He flopped on the ground, crossing his arms behind his head and staring up at the sky. It was a dazzling blue, with thick white banks of clouds, like the ones in old European paintings.

I looked down at him uncertainly. "We'll get sunburned."

He closed his eyes. "No, it's too late in the day. Come on, lie down. Let's take a nap."

I swallowed, nervous. "I don't sleep anymore, remember?" I said.

He shifted slightly in the sun. "So? Lie down."

His eyes were closed. He seemed almost asleep.

"Come on, Luce," he said again, his voice drowsy. He reached out a hand and felt for my leg, tugging me down next to him.

"It's too bumpy," I complained. I could feel pebbles, twigs, rough stalks pressing into my shoulders. "There might be bugs."

"Shhh," Kit said. "It's like the beach." He shifted again, sliding his arm under me. I started to pull away. But his breathing was so slow and steady he had to be falling asleep. And besides, it was comfortable, the soft pressure of his arm behind my head, the warm sun on my face. I listened to the faint trill of the desert around us. Before, that sound had seemed threatening. But now it reassured me – the steady pulse of life where you'd least expect to find it.

I turned toward Kit and I felt him move slightly, accommodating me. Carefully, I leaned my head against his chest. Through the thin fabric of his T-shirt I could hear his heartbeat. For the first time since we'd come to New Mexico, I felt completely safe.

I closed my eyes and slept.

When I opened my eyes, Kit was already awake, squinting at the sky. I started to sit up but he said, "Stay here. This is nice."

So I leaned back against him. "I can't believe I slept," I said into his shirt. "I didn't even dream."

"Yeah, you were out. My arm is completely dead."

"Oh, sorry," I said, starting to get up again.

But Kit grinned and tightened his arm around me. "It's okay. It doesn't matter."

I thought about all those high school girls. Maddie Dilworth, Kristi Bendall, Lara Fitzpatrick. The old girl-friends, new girlfriends, soon-to-be girlfriends. I tried to picture Kit passing me in the hallway at school, in a ragged band of senior boys, smirking and not really looking at me. It made me sad. The last few days had seemed like something outside of time.

"So this is it, right?" I said after a minute. "When we go home, it will be back the way it was. At school, I mean. And everything."

"Well, yeah." He turned to look at me. "It has to. You know?"

It had to. He was a senior. I was Jamie's sister.

Kit reached for my hand, sliding his fingers through mine. "I'm sorry," he said.

I could see in his face that he was. Some people are good at saying they're sorry and some aren't. The ones who aren't say it in a way that makes excuses – "I'm sorry, but…" – or in a way that blames you – "I'm sorry you feel like that" – or in a rush, just to get it over with, because they aren't really sorry at all. But the people who are good at it let you know how bad they feel, and they don't try to protect themselves from how hurt you might be. When Kit said he was sorry, it was like that.

"Is it okay?" he asked.

"Yeah," I said. And it was.

With one finger, I traced his face. Kit leaned closer, his breath soft on my hair. "I like you, Luce. I mean, I really like you."

I smiled at him. "I'm going to tell people I slept with you."

He laughed. "You do that."

"It'll ruin your reputation."

"That *is* my reputation."

I put my hands on either side of his face and held it right above mine. I couldn't see anything but the flecked and speckled depths of his eyes. I didn't regret what had happened with him. Not any of it. With Kit, it was like I'd seen a different part of myself.

"So how come you and I will never end up together?" I asked him.

Kit looked right back at me. "Who says we won't?"

And even though I'd promised myself I wouldn't, I started kissing him again. I held his face in my hands and opened my mouth against his and filled myself with the smell and taste of him. We kissed and kissed. Despite the hard fact of the desert all around us, it was like drowning: a wave of feeling crashing over my head.

But I knew even then that kissing him wasn't what I would miss most. It was falling asleep with him. Somehow, that was the most intimate thing we ever did. And I knew – the way you sometimes sense the future with perfect clarity – that a long time from now, whenever I thought about Kit, that was the moment I'd want back.

38

When we got back to the house, Jamie's bag was on the porch. It looked forlorn and significant. Toronto lay beside it protectively.

Beth was in the living room, on her knees in her spattered work shirt, painting. It startled me to see her exactly as she was when we first met her. She didn't look up when we walked in. Her face was grave with concentration, focused on the work. In steady strokes she brushed turquoise over the metal. I remembered the muffler.

"Hey," I said. "We got something for you."

She looked up. "What?"

"It's in the car. Can you come?"

She set the paintbrush on the edge of the can and followed me outside. When I opened the back door of the car, she smiled. "Where'd you get this?"

"At a gas station, in a pile of junk. It looked like some-thing…" I stopped, feeling shy. "Something you'd like."

"It is." She lifted it deftly from the foot well and banged it against her jeans. We watched the coppery flecks of rust flutter to the ground. I started to close the car door, but she stopped me. She was looking at my sketchbook, which had flopped open on the back seat.

"May I?"

It was the landscape I'd been sketching. I hesitated. "Yeah, I guess."

Beth leaned the muffler against the car and took the sketchbook, studying the scene. She flipped a page. It was the sketch of Kit sleeping. I quickly reached for it, but she stopped me. She turned the drawing slowly, studying it. When she raised her eyes to mine, they were full of understanding. And something else: a kind of pity. "This is it," she said finally, handing the book back. "You drew what you felt."

We stood there, looking at each other, and Beth picked up the muffler, turning it over in her hands as if it were something fragile. "Do you think it's okay to do something stupid – really stupid – once in your life?" she asked.

She was asking me this? I swallowed and stared at the ground. "What do you mean?"

"Is it okay to do one stupid thing? Not because you don't know better, but because you do. And you still can't stop yourself. One mistake. One terrible, wonderful mistake."

Her voice was quiet but fierce. "Is that okay? Are people allowed that?"

It seemed such a small thing when she put it like that. In a whole long life, wasn't a person allowed one mistake?

"I don't know," I said. "It depends on what it is. It depends on who gets hurt."

She was silent. "You're right," she said finally, turning away.

I thought of how Jamie looked at her, the blind, transforming happiness in his face. "Beth," I said, touching her arm. I took a deep breath. "It wasn't a mistake."

Her face softened. "Thank you," she said, climbing the steps to the house.

Jamie was on the phone when we walked in. "It's Dad," he whispered, making a face at me. I sighed. What would we tell him? Maybe the police had already taken care of that for us.

"Really?" Jamie said. "You can? But don't you have to work?" He looked stunned. "You did? Well, that would be … no, that's great. Okay. Yeah, we'll see you there. Here, talk to Luce." He handed the phone over to me with an expression of disbelief.

"Dad?" I pressed the phone to my ear.

"Hi, babe. Listen, I was just telling your brother, I've made reservations for all of us at the Century Resort outside of Albuquerque. I'm taking the rest of the week off."

This was so unexpected I almost dropped the phone. "You're taking off work? But you said you had meetings."

"Yeah," he said. "But I changed things around. I'm on a flight out of Phoenix in a couple of hours. If you drive there tonight, we'll have the rest of the week together."

"So we're not going to Phoenix?"

"It's too far. If you spend another day driving, you'll hardly have any vacation left."

I felt a pang of longing for him, the sureness of his voice, his mind always made up. "Dad, did you talk to the police?"

"I certainly did." He paused. "And your mother."

Mom. I had to call her. And Ginny, too, who'd never believe everything that had happened. They were the lifelines back to my old life.

"It sounds like you've had quite a week," my dad said.

I waited for the inevitable barrage of warnings and advice, the long list of things we should have done differently. But it never came.

"I'm just glad you're all okay. And listen, this is a nice place, babe. Tennis, swimming, golf. We can relax, spend some time together. Sound good?"

"Yes, really good," I said.

"So I'll see you soon?"

"Yeah, Dad. That's great."

I hung up the phone and looked at Jamie, who was shaking his head in amazement. "What's gotten into him?"

"I don't know," I said. "Maybe he misses us."

Jamie gathered the rest of his things in silence. Kit's and mine were still in the car, so we stood awkwardly in the

253

living room, waiting for him. When he came out of the hallway, his face had a stricken look, like he didn't know what to do next. Beth stayed where she was, painting. Jamie kept sending quick glances at her, but she barely looked up when we reached the door. I wondered what they'd said to each other.

"So." Kit swung the door open. The dogs milled in front of it, eager to go out. He gestured at the sculpture. "Maybe we'll see your stuff sometime. At the airport."

Beth finally looked at us. "Maybe you will," she said. She tapped the muffler, which made an echoing clang. "And this, too. I'll find a spot for it."

Jamie stood uncertainly, watching her.

"Drive safe," she said, smiling a little.

She looked at me. "Keep drawing, Lucy," she said. "Maybe I'll see your stuff sometime."

I smiled. "Thanks. Thanks for everything."

"Yeah," Kit said. "Thanks." He looked at Jamie. "Let's go."

Jamie still hesitated, shifting from one foot to the other. Suddenly, he walked across to Beth and bent down behind her, wrapping his arms around her, pressing his face against her neck. Her whole body went rigid for a minute and her paintbrush stopped midstroke. But all she did was lift her free hand and gently touch the side of his face.

Jamie got up, pushing past us, and Kit followed him into the darkening yard. I knelt for a minute by the two dogs, rubbing their ears. "Bye," I whispered to them.

"Bye," Beth called. I heard the quake in her voice.

And then we were on the highway again, the three of us. Kit and Jamie up front. Me in the back, staring out the windshield at the same dark road, through the empty desert, with the mountains hulking along the horizon.

We hadn't gone far when we saw something start to cross the road, just at the edge of the headlights. We all saw it at the same time. Jamie slammed on the brakes, harder than hard, and the tires squealed and the car skidded, angling into the other lane. We were flung forward. The strap of the seat belt cut into my chest. I gripped the back of the front seat, and in the dark I felt Kit's hand touch mine.

But the car stopped.

And there in front of us, frozen in the pool of light, was a coyote. He was thin and gray, scruffy-looking, one paw raised. His narrow face turned toward us, ears pricked, yellow eyes glowing.

He hovered there for a minute, poised in the light, floating like a ghost in the huge, dark desert. Then his foot dropped to the asphalt and he crossed the road, lightly touching the surface. He vanished into the night.

Nobody said anything. We started up again, and Jamie slowly turned the wheel, guiding us back into the lane. In the thick silence of the car, I knew we were all feeling the same thing: grateful for the narrow miss, for the shocking wildness of him, for that small, particular life crossing into the future.

ACKNOWLEDGMENTS

I am indebted to many people for their kind support in the writing of this book. My editor, Christy Ottaviano, is both a thoughtful critic and a staunch advocate, fearlessly encouraging each detour into new territory and helping me find my way. I feel equally lucky to have the support of the staff at Holt, from copyeditors to designers to sales reps, who have worked so hard and often invisibly to give my books their best possible face out in the world. My agent, Steven Malk, has offered helpful counsel throughout the process.

I burdened a handful of readers with a late draft of this manuscript – and little time to read it! – and their smart comments have everywhere improved it. For their diverse perspectives and insights, I'm extremely grateful to Mary Broach, Claire Carlson (and *in absentia,* Claire's mother, Barbara Streeter, for inspiration on the charm bracelet), Laura Forte, Jane Kamensky, Carol Sheriff, and Zoe Wheeler.

A special thanks to my two consultants on police matters: Officer Jack Toomey and especially Chief Fran Hart, who patiently answered endless queries about police procedure and who showed a delightfully unexpected grasp of the demands of the story.

Finally, I thank my family, the guiding stars in my night sky – my husband, Ward Wheeler, and my children, Zoe, Harry, and Grace.